His Perfect Gift

L.L. Diamond

His Perfect Gift

By L.L. Diamond

Published by L.L. Diamond

Cover design by L.L. Diamond/Diamondback Covers

Cover photos: Regency woman wearing a white muslin dress and a long spencer in a Baroque room by Kathy SG and Big Translucent Christmas snowflake in gray colors on transparent background by Olga Moonlight

ISBN-13: 978-1-7373356-4-1

Facebook: https://www.facebook.com/LLDiamond

Instagram: @l.l.diamond

Twitter: @LLDiamond2

Blog: http://lldiamondwrites.com/

Austen Variations: http://austenvariations.com/

Other works by L.L. Diamond include:

Rain and Retribution

A Matter of Chance

An Unwavering Trust
The Earl's Conquest
Particular Intentions
Particular Attachments
Unwrapping Mr. Darcy
It's Always Been You
It's Always Been Us
It's Always Been You and Me
Undoing
Confined with Mr. Darcy
He's Always Been the One
Agony and Hope
His Perfect Gift

Another move and unexpected trials
and stress accompanied the completion of this book.
I owe a huge thank you and hug to everyone who offered
advice, aid, to bring me "wine and chocolates,"
or even be a "DD" if I needed one.
I have the immense fortune of amazing friends and incredible
new neighbors, who have adopted us
into their fold without reservation.
My family, as always, rose to the occasion
and are a huge support.
I couldn't ask for more.
Love to all of you!

Chapter 1

December 16th 1811

Fitzwilliam Darcy dropped his head back into the squabs of the carriage with a sigh. The last thing he desired was to journey across town. Why had he capitulated so easily? He raised his head and levelled as stern a glare as he could muster at Richard. "I must insist you tell me where we are going."

His cousin, who sat across from him, grinned and crossed his arms over his chest. The lout had to enjoy being insufferable. Why else would he behave so? "My, but you are ill-tempered this morning. What has you in such a foul mood these days? I thought your stay with Bingley was to be a remedy, not make matters worse." Richard tried his nerves more often than not, but Darcy refused to let on the true reason for his displeasure.

"If I am ill-tempered, why would two months in a house with Bingley's sister improve my disposition?" When he awakened this morning, he had not expected he would be journeying to Cheapside today. At Richard's first mention of the trip, he had refused, but his cousin, a colonel in the Regulars, was quite adept at picking and picking until Darcy relented. His cousin had not learnt the art in the army, but instead, from the years they had spent together in their youth. All Darcy had wanted was for Richard to cease his torment, which meant he now sat in a carriage bound for Cheapside, of all places.

"Are you not aware how much I dislike the balls and the dinner parties of the Season? I have endured Miss Bingley's daily presence for months, as well as that infernal ball at

Netherfield, and now your mother has insisted upon prolonging my torture by demanding my presence at her Twelfth Night *fête*. Then, I have been invited to a dinner party given by none other than Miss Bingley—as if I have not had enough of her cloying remarks and fawning compliments. I should think those upcoming two events alone would be enough to sour anyone's disposition." Darcy steered his attention to the view outside the window. What he would not give to avoid any further discourse on the subject. He needed Richard to give him quarter.

A hearty chuckle came from across the carriage. "I admit the lady is not well-liked, but the only teeth set on edge by Miss Bingley belong to you, cousin, and I daresay 'tis your own fault."

Darcy's head jerked back. "My fault?"

Richard shifted his sabre and relaxed further into the seat. "You are too concerned with offending Bingley to treat his sister as you would most ladies. You grit your teeth and accept her attentions when you should be as intolerable to her as you are to the others."

He inhaled in an attempt to soothe that well of pressure building in his gut. "I may not enjoy speaking with the ladies as you do, but I am not intolerable." Truth be told, he had only ever enjoyed speaking to one lady, Miss Elizabeth Bennet, and today, his cousin dragged him away from his library to Cheapside. Cheapside of all places! He had refused, if for no other reason than to avoid another reminder of the lady who consumed his thoughts of late. Her uncle lived in Cheapside, did he not? Was there nothing that would spare him the torment of her memory? Unfortunately, his cousin would not leave him to the solitude of his library and had pestered him. Why could Richard not leave him be?

The colonel barked out a laugh. "I beg to differ. I have known many a lady who was offended by your method of keeping them at bay."

"I have no wish to be ensnared by any of them, so I ensure I do nothing to encourage their hopes." With a heavy exhale, Darcy grimaced. "But I am afraid my latest endeavour to be of aid to Bingley has not helped the matter with Miss Bingley."

His cousin lifted his eyebrows and leaned forward in his seat. "So, you have saved Bingley from himself once again? What was it this time? Another bad investment opportunity?"

Darcy shook his head. "Bingley became enamoured of a local girl while in Hertfordshire."

"That does not sound too dire," said Richard, dismissing it with a wave. "He is always fancying himself in love. The notion passes soon enough."

Again, Darcy shook his head. "No, this time was different. Bingley showed a decided preference for the young lady from the first evening of their acquaintance, and by the ball, it had become evident that he had raised the expectations of the neighbourhood. They all believed him soon to propose."

His cousin furrowed his brows. "You felt a marriage to this lady to be imprudent?"

Darcy closed his eyes. How could he forget the deplorable behaviour of Mrs. Bennet and the three youngest Bennet daughters? "The match would have been unwise. She had little fortune, no connections, and the behaviour of her family was objectionable, to say the least."

"You must consider it a triumph to have successfully separated the two."

"You can be certain." Darcy fidgeted with his cuffs, adjusting them at his wrists. "My only regret is that by colluding with Miss Bingley, she seems assured I will propose. I tell you: I am at my wit's end. She is unbearable."

Richard stared at him, his eyes boring into Darcy. What was he about? He could not suspect anything amiss, could he? He straightened and adjusted the set of his shoulders. His cousin started to point his finger, wagging it at Darcy. "Come to think of it, you returned from Netherfield in a horrid mood." A ludicrous, crooked grin lit his cousin's face. "Did you make the acquaintance of a lady in Hertfordshire? Would you be pining for someone as unsuitable as Bingley's new angel?"

He scoffed as he picked a piece of invisible fluff from the sleeve of his topcoat. Elizabeth Bennet? Unsuitable? If not for her family and connections, she would be eminently suitable. "You are ridiculous. I would never be so careless."

His cousin sighed. "No, I suppose you would not." Richard's voice turned dull with the last. Would he prefer Darcy fall in love with a lady their family would never accept?

No, he needed to distract Richard before he guessed the truth of the matter. "So, what is so special about this wine and brandy merchant?"

"Father has raved of the man for a few years now, and I happened to make his acquaintance last summer. I am unsure of his sources, but he boasts of a particularly fine assortment of Port, claret, and French brandy." Richard had dipped his chin a bit with the mention of the last two. The man was certain to be a smuggler or was in partnership with one. "My father was impressed by their selection. He has also advised me to invest in the business, which has yielded a substantial return. Since you enjoy fine spirits as well as a sound business opportunity, I thought you may wish to meet the proprietor."

Darcy suppressed a smile at the success of his manoeuvre. "I do not see the urgency of such a matter. I have a perfectly adequate supplier on Piccadilly Street, whom I have used since my father passed."

With a huff, Richard sat back against the squabs. "I would wager this man's prices to be more reasonable. He also delivers to Mayfair and Belgravia, which means you should not have to return once you have set up an account. Father merely pens him a letter with what he desires, and Mr. Gardiner arranges the rest."

They stared at each other for a few seconds until Richard shook his head. "Whether you decide to do business with him or not, I have made the introduction, thus you cannot fault me for never doing so." He turned towards the window, seeming to watch the buildings pass. Richard rarely lost his good humour. Perhaps Darcy was a bit churlish.

A row of houses along Gracechurch Street drew Darcy's particular interest. He had no desire to argue any further with his cousin. A maid with several children stood upon the steps of a large corner house that appeared to be well kept. Could one of these homes belong to the uncle of Elizabeth Bennet? He had never thought to study the neighbourhood in the past—not that he ventured to Cheapside often, but some of these homes were on 24-foot-wide lots and, with their detailing, could have been nestled between the homes on Mayfair without standing apart. He shook himself. He needed to stop this ridiculousness. The appearance of a house rarely corresponded to the personality of the owner. After all, Longbourn was a charming and well-tended home by all outward appearances, yet the Bennets' coarseness in company belied any impression one may have derived from their first glimpse of the estate.

A small park ahead caught his eye. Had Miss Elizabeth ever walked and enjoyed that particular prospect? She and Miss Bennet claimed to stay with their aunt and uncle from time to time, so the idea was not out of the realm of possibility. With her love for the activity, she must have taken a ramble through the pathways during one of her visits. He could almost envision her strolling through the trees, the hem of her morning gown stained with grass and dirt—much as she had appeared upon her impromptu arrival at Netherfield to care for her sister.

They drew closer, and a young lady standing at the front gates came into focus. He blinked. Was that...? He looked again. The lady was indeed Jane Bennet. Darcy drew back from the window while she entered the park, hand in hand with a small child, a servant trailing behind.

He would have to ensure Bingley remained away from Cheapside for the near future. They had struggled so to prevent his return to Hertfordshire and to conceal Miss Bennet's presence in London; it would not do for him to happen upon her now.

"There is a handsome young lady," said his cousin, causing Darcy to flinch. "You jerked back from the window so. Do you know her?"

With a shrug of his shoulders, Darcy donned a mask of feigned indifference. "I would imagine a tradesman's daughter, one of good means by her gown."

His cousin frowned then narrowed his eyes. "You appeared to have recognised her, or at least, taken an interest?"

"No, I am not acquainted with her, and as for her being of interest..." His last view as they passed was that of Jane Bennet, smiling to the child at her side. "She smiles too much."

Richard gave a great guffaw. "That has to be the most preposterous notion I have ever heard you utter. What man has not been bewitched by the smile of a beautiful woman?"

Miss Elizabeth again came to mind, and Darcy could not help one side of his lip from tugging upward. "Perhaps a pair of fine eyes may one day garner my notice."

His cousin shook his head. "I pity you when they do. You are so accustomed to maintaining your distance, you will be at a loss as to how to win her favour." He turned serious and held Darcy's eye. "But, she will be a lucky woman—a lucky woman indeed." Before Darcy could respond, Richard started. "Oh! We have arrived."

Once the step was placed, Darcy alighted after his cousin and gave a cursory glance to his surroundings. The street in both directions was busy with carts moving their wares. The narrow pavement boasted of a number of people, entering and exiting various shops with their parcels. A milliner was to one side of the door Richard approached, a dressmaker's establishment to the opposite. As he followed his cousin into the shop, the cool air of the room held a slight musty quality. With the exception of the front window, bottles lined the walls, even behind the counter, except where room had been made for a door.

"Colonel! I had not expected to see you today." The man who approached wore a genial countenance, his arms outstretched in a manner that conveyed welcome.

"I have extolled the many virtues of your shop to my cousin, so I thought I would force him from his study to accompany me. He prefers to hide away in his library rather than possibly come in contact with the sun."

Darcy lifted his eyes to the ceiling, which the man saw but laughed. "Cousin, why do you not introduce me?" he said. Regardless of whether he wanted to be there, he would not be rude.

"Fitzwilliam Darcy, may I introduce Mr. Edward Gardiner?"

"You have come at an opportune moment. I just had a new shipment in this morning," said Mr. Gardiner once they had bowed. He lifted an eyebrow to Richard. "I have yet to open it. Would you care to join me? I am certain there is something you would enjoy in those crates."

His cousin rubbed his hands together in a manner more fitting Bingley than a colonel. "Lead the way, my good man."

With a smile, Mr. Gardiner motioned for them to follow him behind the counter. "What do you prefer to drink, Mr. Darcy?"

"I keep a great deal of Port in my cellar. I do stock brandy when I have the opportunity."

Mr. Gardiner nodded. After he said a few words to a man in the office, he led them down a narrow hallway and down a set of stone stairs. The air became more stagnant and stale and tickled his nose as they ventured further. When they reached the bottom, candles lit the musty, windowless chamber where several crates stood in the middle of the stone floor. Racks also lined the high walls, all laden with bottles.

Darcy pulled an unfamiliar bottle from the rack. "Constantia wine?" he said, his eyes wide.

"Is that a favourite, Mr. Darcy?"

He shook his head. "No, I have never tasted it. Do you sell a great deal of it?"

Mr. Gardiner tipped his head one way then the other. "A bit. The Prince Regent purchases part of my stock, as does the colonel's father. The Duke of Devonshire and the Duke of Cumberland have also requested cases. I do not often receive shipments of Constantia wine[i], and it never lasts for long after it arrives." As Darcy made to return the bottle to the shelf, Mr. Gardiner pressed the wine back towards him. "Pray, try it with my compliments."

Darcy shook his head. "'Tis generous of you, sir, but 'tis too much." Constantia wine had to be imported from the southernmost peninsula of Africa and was rare. The bottle Mr. Gardiner offered him was exceedingly expensive.

With a smile, the man retrieved a tool hanging upon the wall. "I sent word to those who purchase my Constantia wine shipments yesterday. Those bottles will be gone within the next few days, and at a substantial price. I am happy to provide you with a bottle to sample. Pray, take it and enjoy."

He gaped at the costly wine. "Thank you. I shall save this for a special occasion."

The man smiled as he pried the tops from the crates. Richard dove into the packing, pulling out bottles and handing them to Mr. Gardiner. "My father would like a couple of bottles of this," said his cousin, holding a bottle closer to a candle.

Darcy set the wine on a table and took a bottle of the brandy his cousin offered him. "I know the seal on this one. My father used to keep a supply of this before the war."

After a waggle of his eyebrows and a crooked grin, his cousin pulled another bottle from the straw. "How many would you like?"

How many, indeed. Darcy set the bottles he wished to purchase to one side with the Constantia wine until they had emptied the contents of the crates. Then, Mr. Gardiner tasked a boy with packing Darcy's order as well as Richard's before they returned to the office upstairs. Before Mr. Gardiner could close the door behind him, a feminine hand wrapped around the edge.

"Uncle, my aunt sent me to ask when you would be home for dinner."

Wait! He knew that voice. When the door opened, Miss Elizabeth Bennet stood in the doorway. Her cheeks were a bit pink, possibly from the chill of the day, and her celestial blue pelisse brought out the same colour flecks in her eyes. Of all the places in Cheapside, Richard had to bring him to Miss Elizabeth's uncle?

Her eyes darted to him and widened. "Mr. Darcy?"

After they bowed, his cousin stepped forward. "Miss Elizabeth, I did not know you were in town, or else I would have called upon you. As I recall, you do enjoy walking in that small park just down the street."

Darcy swallowed the "Hah!" that threatened to burst from his chest. He had been correct about her penchant for walking.

Elizabeth dipped her chin. "I do. How good of you to remember, Colonel." Her eyes darted back to Darcy.

"I hope you and your family are well?" Darcy asked.

"They are well. I thank you."

Mr. Gardiner grinned and clasped his hands before him. "I had wondered if you were the Mr. Darcy who lately visited Hertfordshire. I have heard much of you from my nieces—and my sister, Mrs. Bennet."

He tore his eyes from Miss Elizabeth, then glanced at Richard, who grinned from ear to ear. "Yes, I met the Bennets while I stayed with my friend Bingley."

The man's smile faltered just a hair before Miss Elizabeth turned back to his cousin. "How is your father, Colonel? Though it has been some time, I enjoyed making his acquaintance."

Darcy almost swayed in his spot. Elizabeth Bennet had met his uncle. She appeared to know Richard. How had he been unaware of this?

"Colonel, Mr. Darcy, we would be pleased if you would join us for dinner? While Mr. Darcy has met my oldest niece, you have yet to do so," said Mr. Gardiner to his cousin. The man still wore a cheerful expression. Darcy's mouth opened and closed. Why could he not speak?

"What do you say, Darcy? Or have you promised Georgiana you would join her?"

"She is with your mother. I am certain Lady Fitzwilliam will insist she remain until this evening." His sister never arrived home early from a day at the Fitzwilliams'. Their aunt and uncle always insisted on her joining them for their evening meal. Today was not likely to be different.

"Excellent!" His cousin slapped him on the back. "We shall be pleased to join you, Gardiner."

Darcy suppressed the urge to squeeze his eyes closed. He departed Hertfordshire to escape the hold Miss Elizabeth held over him, but here she was, standing before him. How could he spend an entire evening in her company? Richard would notice his unease. His cousin knew him too well to be fooled by those usual devices he employed to avoid a lady's company.

And what of Miss Bennet? Richard would also learn that he lied when they saw her at the park. This was why he hated dissembling, but how could he have known? He grimaced. What a trial this evening would be!

Chapter 2

Elizabeth's mind refused to cease the infernal thoughts and questions that turned over and over, refusing her a moment's peace. Why was Mr. Darcy in Cheapside? He appeared as proud and haughty as in Meryton, which was a marked contrast to his cousin. Elizabeth could not credit the two were related, though she should know how different two relations could be. After all, her uncle and her mother were nothing alike. Jane and Lydia had quite disparate personalities, as well.

When she entered the parlour, her aunt looked up from her embroidery. "Well?"

"He requested dinner be at six, and he has invited Colonel Fitzwilliam and Mr. Darcy to join us."

Her aunt gave a heavy exhale and stood. "Well, he is a fine one for surprises, is he not?"

While her aunt disappeared down to the kitchen to speak to the cook, Elizabeth turned towards the window. Her foot tapped in an incessant rhythm, and she bit her thumbnail. The carriages and people all passed as though they had not a care in the world. Meanwhile, she had the prideful Mr. Darcy to contend with this evening. What had made him accept the invitation? Would he not believe her uncle and aunt beneath him thus unworthy of his notice? He had treated those in Hertfordshire in such a way. It was not difficult to believe he would behave in much the same fashion here.

"Thank goodness for Mrs. Smith. She has a couple of chickens she can roast, as well as some potatoes. I believe that should be enough." Aunt Gardiner straightened her skirt as she bustled back to her chair near the fire.

"You behave as though they will each eat an entire bird by themselves."

"You can never be too careful when you are entertaining," said her aunt, pointing a finger in Elizabeth's direction. "One day, you may be in a similar predicament, then we shall see who is laughing."

"You forget I shall likely never marry, Aunt. I shall embroider cushions and teach Jane's many children to play the pianoforte very ill indeed." What else could one expect of a lady who was merely tolerable?

"What is this nonsense?" Aunt Gardiner shook her head. "You are a handsome young lady. I believe you will find a gentleman who appreciates your accomplishments."

"We shall see."

Her aunt set down her embroidery. "Does this have to do with Mr. Darcy? You must not let that comment at the assembly bother you so. You forget that I met the young man when he was but a boy. He was always quiet and reserved, yet he never failed to be polite. I do believe something must have been amiss for him to have made such a statement that evening."

How like Jane she sounded! "Or he could have changed since you knew him. As you said, he was a boy at the time."

Aunt Gardiner shook her head. "Such extreme alterations are rare. His father was a fine man. I am certain the son will be just like him."

The door opened and the children rushed inside with a harried Jane following. "Mama! 'Tis cold outside," said six-year-old Jemima. "Do you think it will snow for Christmastide?"

With a smile, her aunt took Jemima's pink little hands, removed her gloves, and warmed them in her own. "I do not know. I am sure it is possible, but the weather would need to be even colder for snow."

"Even colder?" Jemima's little eyes were huge while she spoke in an awed voice.

Jane smiled and gestured for Jemima to come to her. "Come, dearest. Let us take you to your nurse to put you to rights. I am sure your younger brothers will be awake from their naps and you will be having dinner soon."

Eight-year-old Beatrice ran ahead while Jemima walked in a prim manner to Jane and took her hand. "I hope Mrs. Smith has made biscuits. The twins like biscuits."

"Well, if you are good and eat all of your dinner, perhaps your nurse will have a biscuit for you too." A tiny gasp came from Jemima, making Elizabeth smile. The little girl possessed a child-like wonder she envied. How lovely to see the world through the innocent eyes of a child—one who had never been told she was tolerable.

She grimaced. How would she endure an entire evening spent in the company of Mr. Darcy? What she would not give to fall ill between now and dinner!

"I must thank you for the wonderful meal, Mrs. Gardiner. I know we must have been an imposition to be added at the last minute," said Mr. Darcy in an earnest tone.

The meal had been wonderful, as always. After they dined, Mr. Gardiner and the gentlemen spoke over Port and cigars until they joined the ladies in the drawing room.

Elizabeth kept her head down but lifted her eyebrows. Who was this man? He was certainly not the Mr. Darcy she had been in company with in Hertfordshire. Had he been taking lessons in amiability from his cousin?

"I must also convey my appreciation for being included in your lovely party," said the colonel. He glanced at Jane, who pinked, but not in the same manner as when Mr. Bingley smiled at her. Her sister was lost to Mr. Bingley, which made the gentleman's sisters hideous creatures—even Mr. Darcy had been more gracious in her aunt and uncle's home than Miss Bingley and Mrs. Hurst.

When she lifted her head, Mr. Darcy stared at her, his eyes boring into her with the same intensity as Hertfordshire. What could he mean by looking at her so? "Mr. Darcy, I understand when you departed Hertfordshire, you were eager to see your sister. I hope she is well."

His brow furrowed. "She is quite well. If you would not mind, I should like to introduce her to you while you are in town. I can bring her here or you could have tea with her at Darcy House."

"I do not know what to say." She was not lying. He never seemed to think much of her, and now he wanted her to make the acquaintance of his sister? "I am certain whatever is easier for her will do. I would not wish her uneasy by being in an unfamiliar place."

He glanced about the room. "I am certain she would enjoy meeting your aunt and your cousins. Her favourite part of visiting the tenants at Pemberley is the children."

"She finds them less intimidating than the adults," said the colonel. "She is terribly shy, but the children run to her upon her arrival and call to their parents. By the time the mothers approach, Georgiana has told the children the reason for her call. They then speak for her. I believe she could go an entire visit without ever needing to speak to an adult." Shy? Mr. Wickham claimed her terribly proud! Would the colonel tell a falsehood about his own cousin? He did not seem as though he would.

"How old is Miss Darcy?" asked Jane.

Mr. Darcy's gaze shifted from her to her sister. "She is not yet sixteen."

Her aunt dipped her chin and gave a pointed look to Elizabeth. "How good of her to take on that responsibility at such a young age."

"I have never pushed her or tried to persuade her to take on a mistress's duties, but she insisted upon learning two years ago. My housekeeper began her instruction, but with her recent stay in London, her companion and the housekeeper in town are continuing her education."

Her aunt sat straight with her hands in her lap, the picture of a perfect hostess. "As I recall, your mother was quite accomplished at the pianoforte. Has your sister learnt the art?"

Mr. Darcy's brow furrowed. "Your husband mentioned you hailed from Derbyshire, but I was not aware you knew my mother."

"Oh, yes," said Aunt Gardiner. "My father built Heathersage—"

"I know Heathersage. 'Tis close in size to the Miss Bennets' home. Your father was Mr. Matthew Campbell."

"Yes, sir."

The gentleman's eyes lit. "I remember my father was a great admirer of your father's horseflesh. My first horse was purchased from your father." How he sounded like one of the children when the possibility of sweets was mentioned. "Your grandfather purchased the land and started raising horses before your father had the manor house built. He was an excellent man. I was terribly sorry to hear of his death."

"Thank you." Aunt Gardiner nodded. "My brother has carried on with breeding horses as my father taught him."

"Your family was rather large, was it not?" asked the colonel.

"There were twelve of us. I have a brother in the army and two in the navy, and two who took orders. My sisters have all made respectable matches."

Uncle Gardiner grinned while he looked upon his wife with a soft expression. "I fear she disappointed the lot when she married me. Her brother had intended to match her with one of his friends from Oxford."

"But I have never regretted it." Her aunt smiled. "We intend to journey to the Lakes this summer. I look forward to breaking our journey at Heathersage. Lizzy is to accompany us.

I hope to introduce her to my friends and family during our stay."

Mr. Darcy's vivid blue eyes latched onto her once again. She should be accustomed to his staring by now, but the intensity of his gaze caused butterflies to take flight within the confines of her stomach. How would she sit for the remainder of the evening without shifting constantly in her chair? "You must tell me when you are to visit. I would be pleased to invite you to dinner at Pemberley during your stay."

Jane clasped her hands together. "Oh! How lovely!"

"We thank you for your kind invitation," said her aunt.

"Be careful, Mr. Darcy," said her uncle. "My wife has expressed the wish on more than one occasion to see Pemberley. She will be applying to the housekeeper for a tour if you are not careful."

Mr. Darcy's gaze returned to Aunt Gardiner. "You have no need to apply to my housekeeper. I would be happy to show you my home. I am certain Georgiana could be of aid to me. She may know some of Mrs. Reynolds' anecdotes or the history of some of the rooms or furniture I do not."

"Miss Bennet, how long are you to be in town?" asked Colonel Fitzwilliam.

"We have no fixed plans to depart." Jane glanced to her aunt then Elizabeth. "We are at the whim of our aunt and uncle."

"Mr. Gardiner and I hope they will pass Christmastide with us. Of course, their father does not tolerate too long an absence from Lizzy. He could pen a letter at any time if he desires their return, but I do hope they shall stay for a while.

The children adore them, and we enjoy their society, do we not?" She looked to her husband, who nodded.

"Indeed we do. My business will take me near Drury Lane in a few days. We thought to take the girls to the theatre during their stay; my wife always purchases them a gown or two, and we take them to Hatchard's for a book. I have also arranged for a piano master to give Lizzy lessons while she is here."

The side of her head prickled where Mr. Darcy's gaze rested. Why could he not stare at someone else? "I do not remember Miss Elizabeth's skill at the pianoforte as lacking, by any means, but I am certain she will only improve with the aid of a master. I look forward to hearing the results."

Elizabeth's eyes met his for but a moment before she dropped her gaze to her lap. "Thank you." Why were her cheeks warm? Could she have caught a cold?

"Say, Darcy, do you not have a box for the Season?"

After he cleared his throat, Mr. Darcy blinked and nodded. "I do. If you decide which play you would like to see, I would be pleased to host you. We could have a late supper at Darcy House afterward."

"We would be delighted. Thank you for the invitation," said Uncle Gardiner.

When Elizabeth turned, her aunt watched her. "How wonderful. I am certain we would be thrilled to join you. Would we not, Lizzy?" Her aunt lifted her eyebrows.

"We would indeed." Why was her voice so faint? How mortifying!

The colonel engaged Jane in conversation, but Elizabeth was across the room and could not hear the low tones of their discourse. Instead, she was forced to join her aunt and uncle's discussion of Derbyshire with Mr. Darcy. First, Mr. Darcy joined them for dinner, and now, they were to accompany Mr. Darcy to the theatre. Was she to spend her entire stay in London in the society of Mr. Darcy? Whatever grievous sin had she committed to deserve such a fate?

Chapter 3

The moment the carriage pulled away from the kerb, Richard began to laugh while he shook his head. "I cannot believe I am saying this, but you lied to me. You told me a falsehood. When we passed Miss Bennet in the park, you claimed her unknown to you." He pointed straight at Darcy's chest. "You dissembled." That dratted finger began to bob up and down. "And I am willing to wager all I own—"

"Which is not much—"

"How much I own is beside the point. As I was saying, I am willing to wager my meagre assets that Miss Bennet is Bingley's latest angel, the one you are proud of yourself for separating from him, but why you believe her unsuitable is a mystery. Her manners are impeccable, and she seems to be goodness itself."

Darcy groaned and raked his fingers through his hair. "Miss Bennet alone is not objectionable, but her mother is atrocious. She all but announced a betrothal to all and sundry at the ball at Netherfield. While I cannot prove a thing, I believe she told Miss Bennet to journey to Netherfield on horseback for dinner with Bingley's sisters when the entire neighbourhood was aware at sunrise that it would rain. Her mother is vulgar and loud, and the three younger sisters should not be out—the two youngest in particular. They made more than one scene at Bingley's ball."

His cousin's eyes narrowed and he crossed his arms over his chest. "How does their behaviour differ from some of the families of the *ton*? Lady Chesterfield has announced her intention to ensnare you for one of her daughters on several occasions, yet you remain unwed. You have never so much as stood up with one of them."

"And I never will," he said with a shudder. Lady Chesterfield's daughters were as insufferable as their mother. With their flirtatious manners, they were an embarrassment. Was it the oldest who leaned forward in an effort to show him her bosom, but ended up falling face first onto the floor? He had disappeared into the crush of the ball before the mother could claim he ripped her gown. "As for Bingley, I had concerns Mrs. Bennet would force Miss Bennet to accept him."

"Again, Cousin, how is her behaviour any different from the mamas of the *ton*? Anne has no desire to marry you, but our aunt would have her standing before the altar if you finally surrendered to her incessant nagging."

"Very well, I accept your chastisement. Does that please you?"

"Not just yet," said Richard, entirely too happy for Darcy's taste. "I want to know about Miss Elizabeth."

Darcy squeezed his eyes closed for a moment before he reopened them. Damn and blast!

"I have never witnessed you behave so with a lady. How the poor thing did not catch aflame at how you watched her. She was exceedingly ill-at-ease with the attention too. For some reason, she does not like you."

His head shot up from consulting his pocket watch. "I beg your pardon?" What could Richard mean? Miss Elizabeth flirted and bantered with him at Netherfield. Why would he believe she was ill-at-ease with him?

Richard's eyes widened. "You did not know, did you?"

"She flirted with me when her sister was ill at Netherfield. We oft times traded barbs at the expense of Miss Bingley. I know Miss Elizabeth found her as disagreeable as I do."

"I have no doubt Miss Elizabeth found great humour at the expense of Miss Bingley," said Richard. "I have met her two or three times, and she has a manner about her. She studies people and their personalities. On more than one occasion this evening, she tilted her head and watched you when you were not looking, with a small line between her eyebrows. I believe you confuse her a great deal."

"But why do you think she dislikes me?"

"Could you not tell she was uncomfortable? Perhaps because I know her to be a friendly sort, I recognised that she stared at her lap more than she would look at you. She was also quieter than is her wont. I assume you were your usual charming self in Hertfordshire, but did you treat her as you do most ladies?"

Darcy looked away. What had he said to Bingley at the assembly? His head dropped back against the squabs. "The moment we entered the assembly rooms in Meryton, we could hear the gossip. Bingley's income as well as mine filtered through the room. I had not wanted to be there. I wanted to help Georgiana."

"Georgiana needed my mother. She needed a lady, and thankfully, Mother found Mrs. Annesley. You could do naught but let her have that time. You must admit that my mother was of great benefit to her."

"I cannot deny that Lady Fitzwilliam's counsel and presence did Georgiana a great deal of good." Darcy shook his head. "Regardless of the reason for my ill-temper that evening,

Bingley insisted I go. Mrs. Bennet was obvious in her machinations, and whenever I escaped, I would turn to find Miss Bingley nearby. Bingley danced with Miss Bennet, then he sought me out, insisting I stand up with Miss Elizabeth. He directed my attention to her, and our eyes met. I thought to warn her off."

"What did you say?"

"I said, 'She is tolerable, I suppose, but not handsome enough to tempt me.' I may have also said something of it being a punishment to stand up with her and her being slighted by other men."

Richard snickered and scratched the day's growth of beard upon his cheek. "Have you ever apologised?"

"No, but when we were in company, she would challenge me." He frowned. "She never behaved as though she disliked me."

"Are you certain?"

Darcy threw up his hands. "I do not know. Perhaps I had the wrong of it. I thought she welcomed my attention."

"You have closed yourself away for far too long, Cousin." With a sigh, Richard watched him for a minute. "If you carry a *tendre* for the lady, you should beg her forgiveness and court her."

He sat up straight and gave an incredulous bark. "Court her? What of your parents and Lady Catherine? Do you expect them to embrace my choice if it is Miss Elizabeth?"

His cousin gave a one-shouldered shrug. "Lady Catherine would never accept anyone but her daughter as your bride, but my parents are not as closed-minded as you may think. Do not forget: they approved of my brother's marriage."

"She came with a fortune of fifty-thousand pounds. Most of the ton has overlooked her father's connection to trade due to such a sum—not to mention your parents' sanction. Miss Elizabeth has one-thousand pounds upon her mother's death."

"But she would have my parents' approval, and did you not hear Mr. Gardiner? He may sell gin and more common spirits in his shop, but he makes most of his money from the great houses of England—the Devonshires, the Prince Regent. He may be a tradesman, but he is a wealthy one."

This time, Darcy crossed his arms over his chest. "A tradesman your father would invite for dinner?"

"He has commented about how they appear as people of fashion. I do not think he would be ashamed to have them in his home. He has mentioned greeting them at the theatre."

"Truly?" asked Darcy. He could not imagine his uncle in company with a tradesman.

"Her father is a gentleman. 'Tis not as if you are attempting to wed a courtesan or a scullery maid."

Darcy covered his face with his hands and let them slide to his chin. "I fled Hertfordshire for fear I would offer for her."

His cousin laughed in that manner that infuriated him. "If you had offered for her, I daresay she would have turned you down without a second thought. Despite her situation, she has a certain amount of pride. She would never wed for the mere notion of security. Her uncle has even mentioned that she hopes to marry for love."

With his cousin's last words, Darcy fell silent. All this time, he assumed she sought his attention. Could she have been arguing with him in earnest? Bingley had wished for them to cease their feisty discussion when her sister was ill at Netherfield. Had he noticed what Darcy had not?

Their arrival at Darcy House startled him from his reverie. After they alighted, Watson ushered them inside and out of the chill of the evening. He took their coats and hats, then disappeared into the servants' passages.

A lilting melody drew them to the music room where Georgiana sat at her pianoforte, engrossed in the music sheets before her. She had grown so in the past few years and more resembled a young lady than a girl, though she was still very young. He could have killed Wickham when he set eyes on him in Meryton. Georgiana had such a trusting and naïve heart. The injury he inflicted was of the acutest kind.

"Brother!" She jumped up from the instrument and hurried to him. "I am so pleased you have returned."

"When did you arrive home?" he asked.

"Oh, only a short time ago. Lady Fitzwilliam and a maid escorted me. I have been practicing ever since." She glanced between them. "Did you and Richard visit your club?"

"No," he shook his head, "our cousin wished to introduce me to someone. As it happens, I am acquainted with the gentleman's nieces. I would like you to make their acquaintances. I told Mrs. Gardiner we would call on the morrow as long as you had no fixed plans.

Georgiana regarded him with her eyebrows raised. "You hope to marry one of them." They both turned at Richard laughing beside them.

"Forgive me, but I had not expected her to be so intuitive." He waved a hand. "Do not order a new gown yet, Poppet, the lady in question is far from enamoured of your brother."

His sister was unperturbed. She perked up with an ever-so-slight smile. "Well, we must remedy that, must we not? So long as she is nothing like Miss Bingley, that is."

"God forbid!" Darcy shuddered, making Georgiana giggle. "She is nothing like Miss Bingley and finds the lady as ridiculous as we do."

She grasped his hands. "Then I must make this lady's acquaintance. Do you think she will like me?"

"I am certain she will," said Richard. "She will find you charming indeed."

"Do you truly think so?"

Darcy smiled and shoved down the urge to tousle her hair as he did when she was small. "I have no doubts." He squeezed her hands. "I was told this evening that her aunt and uncle have hired a piano master for her while she is in town. You could invite her here to play if you like."

"Does she play well?"

"She is not as skilled as you, yet I have heard few who can match her for expression." The feeling she imbued into the music made up for her lack of formal instruction. Few enchanted him as she did when she played and sang.

"Well then, I must ensure she becomes my sister. Mrs. Annesley and I were to work with Mrs. Hendricks on household duties, but we can do so when I return."

"I assure you, calling on Miss Elizabeth will be much more pleasurable than learning household duties," said Richard with an exaggerated grimace.

"Miss Elizabeth?" Georgiana's eyes darted back to him. "Is this the Miss Elizabeth Bennet you mentioned in your letters from Hertfordshire?"

His cousin rubbed his hands together with a wide grin. "Do tell. He never made mention of her in my letters."

"Perhaps because I knew you would behave in such an absurd manner." Why did he allow Richard a room in his house? If he insisted upon Richard residing with his parents, Darcy could have him removed from the house. That would be one way to shut his mouth.

"You should not call me absurd when I can help you." Lord, but he hated when Richard spoke in that sing-song fashion, like he was a child.

"How would you help me?"

He waggled his eyebrows. "I can help you win the fair Miss Elizabeth."

Darcy scoffed and rolled his eyes. "If I succeed in my suit, I would prefer to know she accepted me for me. I shall not dissemble."

Georgiana clasped her hands in front of her. "Well said. When shall we call upon Miss Elizabeth?"

"Tomorrow at eleven, so we must leave in time to journey to Cheapside." She gave no indication of dismay when he mentioned their destination.

"I shall wear my best day gown and be ready."

He blew out a noisy breath. Was his cousin correct? Would Lord and Lady Fitzwilliam support him if he wed Miss Elizabeth? But what if his cousin was correct and Miss Elizabeth carried a poor opinion of him? He would need to change her mind. The problem was he had no idea how to court a lady—how to please a lady worthy of being pleased. What was he to do?

Chapter 4

Another carriage passed the front window, disappearing around the corner into the thick, grey mist. The day had dawned with a damp chill and dense fog that seemed to envelop the people who walked along the pavement, as though once they ventured too far, they vanished into nothingness. Elizabeth bit her thumbnail and tapped her foot.

"Watching and fretting will not make them arrive any sooner."

She whirled around to face her aunt. "Why do you believe I desire their presence?"

A small smile crept across her aunt's features. "You have not left that window for the past hour."

Elizabeth huffed. She adored her aunt, but at times, her open nature could be more frustrating than someone who never spoke a word. "Despite his amiability last night, I still maintain that Mr. Darcy is a prideful and disagreeable man. I am merely bored and desirous of something to watch outside. If not for the mist, I could see the park down the street and not just the shadow of the trees."

"Mr. Darcy honours you by his request to introduce you to his sister. He has singled you out and hinted of his interest."

Interest? Her aunt could not possibly be correct. He looked upon her with disdain and judgement. He watched her to find fault. What had he said at the assembly? She was tolerable and not handsome enough to tempt him. "I told you what he said of my appearance. He would never court a lady he found unattractive."

Her aunt continued the even stitches of her embroidery without looking up from her work. "Men say all sorts of nonsense to one another. What they actually believe is another matter. The man who attended dinner last night is taken with you, my dear. When he was not engaged in conversation with another member of our party, he watched your every response. I assure you—he finds you much more than tolerable."

"I agree with my aunt," said Jane as she closed the parlour door behind her. "Did he not ask to stand up with you more than once?"

"He requested a set at Lucas Lodge, but he never asked another lady that evening. I do not believe he truly wanted to dance."

"Then why would he ask?" Jane lifted her eyebrows.

"Sir William Lucas put me forward as a 'very desirable partner.' I am certain Mr. Darcy felt obligated."

Aunt Gardiner scoffed. "If he had not wished for a set, do you think a suggestion would force him to do so? After all, he refused Mr. Bingley at the assembly, and he is the gentleman's closest friend."

A knock at the front door made Elizabeth jump and turn back to the window. An expensive carriage with a pair of matching greys now stood near the kerb where nothing had been before.

Her hand clutched at her stomach. Would Miss Darcy be as proud and disagreeable as her brother? Mr. Wickham claimed she was, but the colonel, Miss Darcy's own cousin, described her as shy. Which description was accurate? She had never known the colonel to dissemble.

"Lizzy, come away from the window," said her aunt. "Broome will be showing in the Darcys at any moment."

She joined her aunt at the sofa and then fidgeted with the folds of her skirt until the door opened. "Mr. and Miss Darcy."

Once they entered, Mr. Darcy nodded and shifted to the side. "Miss Georgiana Darcy, may I introduce Mrs. Gardiner and her nieces Miss Bennet and Miss Elizabeth."

The girl curtseyed as they returned the civility. "I am pleased to make your acquaintance," she said. Her hands were clasped before her, each gripping the other until her white knuckles stood out in contrast to the pink of her skin. She took a step closer to Elizabeth. "My brother mentioned you in his letters from Hertfordshire. He tells me you play and sing with great feeling." She struggled with the words and glanced to her brother a great deal, as though ensuring she had not spoken out of turn.

"I am flattered to receive such a compliment," said Elizabeth. "I had no idea of your brother's admiration for my performances. I have always considered my own accomplishment with the pianoforte to be ill indeed, though I understand you have a great talent for the instrument. I believe Miss Bingley made mention of it at Netherfield."

Miss Darcy blushed and met Elizabeth's eye for but a moment. "Miss Bingley is too kind in her praise."

"Pray, do be seated." Aunt Gardiner gestured towards the chairs by the fire, but Miss Darcy took the seat beside Elizabeth. The young lady's hands clutched her reticule. The poor dear was terrified. Was she trembling as well?

"I understand you are learning to run your brother's household. How are you faring with the endeavour?"

"Mrs. Reynolds, our housekeeper at Pemberley, and Mrs. Hendricks, our housekeeper here, are patient with me. I must admit I enjoy some tasks more than others. Keeping the household accounts is quite dull." Miss Darcy answered Elizabeth's query well, but she glanced at her brother more than once while she spoke.

Aunt Gardiner smiled in a gentle manner. "Few ladies take pleasure in keeping their accounts, but we know it is a necessary evil. Your brother mentioned you are visiting tenants."

Miss Darcy gave a jerky nod. "I have long tried to do so. My mother faithfully cared for our tenants. Mrs. Reynolds helped me until I was old enough to venture out with a footman and a maid. The children are delightful."

"Lizzy cares for the tenants of Longbourn," said Jane. "She has done so since she was young."

"I remember when she began." Aunt Gardiner's smile grew as she leaned against the arm of her chair. "I believe she was eight when she came running into the house. She had been out on one of her rambles and happened upon a tenant cottage. The little boy who lived there had broken his arm a few days prior, and the break had never been set. She was beside herself."

Miss Darcy's hand went to her chest. "How terrible! Did the boy get help?"

"My father took him to the apothecary in Meryton," said Elizabeth. "Mr. Jones set the break and taught the father how to wrap the arm to keep the bone in place. The break was severe and had been a gruesome spectacle before it was set. Mr. Jones gave him the aid he required. I did little in comparison."

Her gaze met Mr. Darcy's for a second before she diverted her attention back to the sister. Why could she not hold his eye?

"You prevented him from being disfigured," said Mr. Darcy. "While you may believe your actions had little effect, I can assure you, to the father, who required that boy's aid on their farm, bringing his son's plight to the attention of your father was invaluable. That boy will be better able to work his father's farm when he becomes older and support his own family one day. You made an immeasurable difference to his life."

Her cheeks heated. Had Mr. Darcy truly paid her a compliment? "I never considered my actions in such a way. At the time, I think the sight of the boy's arm frightened me, which was why I ran home as fast as I could. He was in terrible pain."

"You were young," said her aunt, "but after, you began walking out to the tenants' houses and speaking to the children, if you will remember. When anything was amiss, you returned to Longbourn and told your father or his steward."

One side of Elizabeth's lips curved. "At least now I can do more than when I was a child. I still find it difficult to credit that my father allowed me to visit tenants at such a young age."

"You were brave to do so on your own." Miss Darcy's voice was soft and her eyes wide.

Elizabeth laughed and shook her head. "I would say I was headstrong, and my father allowed me to do as I pleased. He has always indulged me. My friend Charlotte would accompany me at times. She is seven years my senior and scolded me more than once for how far I would roam without a footman to ensure my safety."

"Has Miss Lucas been well?" said Mr. Darcy.

She turned to him, her stomach tumbling and rolling in an incessant motion. "She is well. She is lately betrothed to my cousin, Mr. Collins."

Mr. Darcy's eyes widened a hairsbreadth. "I had not known they were courting."

"I believe most of Meryton was surprised by the match," said Jane. "Miss Lucas is gratified by the betrothal, as is her family. They wed in early January."

He cleared his throat. "Forgive me. I should be asking you to convey my best wishes in your next letter."

Jane's eyes darted to Elizabeth before she gave a polite smile. "I am certain she will be happy to receive them."

"I shall be sure to include your well wishes the next time I write to her." Elizabeth turned back to Miss Darcy. She could not take much more of that internal fluttering. Dear Lord, she sounded like her mother!

"Mr. Darcy!" Her uncle entered with his usual wide grin, causing them to rise from their seats. "I hope your journey today was easy. The weather is dreadful. I cannot remember the last time we had such a thick mist covering the neighbourhood."

Mr. Darcy stood and bowed before accepting her uncle's proffered hand. "The fog lengthened our trip, but my driver did well with the limited view of the road." He held out his arm towards his sister. "Miss Georgiana Darcy, may I present Mr. Edward Gardiner."

"I am pleased to make your acquaintance," said Miss Darcy in soft tones. Elizabeth frowned. Why would Mr. Wickham claim this young lady proud and disagreeable? Her timid demeanour was obvious to anyone who cared to examine her behaviour. She could scarce look anyone in the eye, with the exception of her brother, and her hands had either gripped something or fidgeted since she arrived. What could Mr. Wickham have meant by telling such a falsehood? For it had to be a falsehood. She had the proof of his lie before her.

As Miss Darcy and Elizabeth sat, Mr. Darcy remained standing. "I hope you do not mind, but I took the liberty of sending a servant to the Theatre Royal. For the next week, they are staging Hamlet as they did in October when the new theatre opened. I have heard the performance is excellent." Mr. Darcy glanced between her and her uncle. "Would Saturday be too soon to attend?"

Uncle Gardiner's eyebrows lifted. "Well, Lizzy, can you make do with a tragedy?"

"Do you not like Hamlet, Miss Elizabeth?" asked Miss Darcy.

Elizabeth rolled her eyes with a slight upturn of her lips. "My uncle teases me since I am more inclined towards comedies than tragedies. As your brother may remember, I dearly love to laugh. But I am not averse to seeing Hamlet. If the production is so well done, then I may become a convert and never read another comedy again." A happy giggle came from Miss Darcy while her uncle shook his head.

"After your father had you read Romeo and Juliet, you refused to read Shakespeare again until he insisted you read Twelfth Night. He had to bribe you with comedies to force you to read the tragedies."

Miss Darcy frowned, and her head hitched back a bit. "Why would he force you to read what you disliked?"

"He wished to discuss them with me. My mother does not read much besides the gossip columns."

"I am not quick-minded enough for Papa's taste," said Jane. "He began teaching Lizzy Shakespeare after she bested him at chess."

The side of her head prickled. She need not look to know Mr. Darcy was watching her. "How old were you?" he asked.

She steeled herself and met his gaze. "I was nine."

His eyebrows lifted. "Do you still play?"

"Papa and my uncle still challenge me when they want to play." She turned her attention back to Miss Darcy. She could not take much more of his intent stare. The havoc his crystalline blue eyes wrought on her insides!

Uncle Gardiner laughed. "Her father and I have a wager on which one of us will finally put her in check mate. She oft times bests me in no more than fifteen moves. She once claimed victory with only eight."

"Do you play chess, Miss Darcy?" She needed to shift the conversation to someone other than herself, lest Mr. Darcy gape at her for the entire call.

The girl turned to her and gave a slight shrug. "I have played my brother, but I do not understand the strategy enough to win." She bit her lip and stiffened. "I would be pleased to have you both call me Georgiana. Perhaps you could join me tomorrow for tea? If so, then I may hear you play and sing too." She became more animated, though her speech came out faster as she moved through the questions.

Elizabeth rested a hand over Miss Darcy's. The poor thing needed to relax. "I shall need to ask my aunt. Since we are her guests, she may have plans for us."

"I must call on Mrs. Jameson tomorrow," said her aunt, "and I know you will not want to join me, so you may do as you like."

Miss Darcy took Elizabeth's hand and squeezed. "Say you will come. We shall have ever so much fun."

Elizabeth could not help but smile at the young lady's enthusiasm. "Very well, I shall come, but if I am to address you as Georgiana, you must call me Lizzy as my sisters do."

"I have always wanted a sister."

She and Jane smiled at each other. "Well, I have four, and at times, I would not mind giving away my younger sisters. You may take all three of them if you wish."

"Lizzy!" chorused Jane and Aunt Gardiner at her impertinence.

Miss Darcy covered her mouth with her hands and giggled. "I have only Fitzwilliam." When she removed her hands, her lips curved as she looked to Mr. Darcy. "But he is the best of brothers."

"You are fortunate to have him." Elizabeth had not lied. A Bennet son would have meant everything to those at Longbourn. She sometimes imagined how different her mother and perhaps Lydia and Kitty would be if a brother had been born to their family.

"I am fortunate indeed."

The obvious affection between brother and sister caused a warm sensation in her chest. She now knew Mr. Wickham lied about Georgiana, but to what end? Was all of his story a falsehood? If so, perhaps her impression of him was incorrect. But did that mean her first impression of Mr. Darcy was flawed as well? The revelation of it all was enough to make her mind spin in a dizzying motion.

Chapter 5

The Gardiners' home had bustled with activity from the moment Darcy had stepped through the door. As soon as he had arrived, the butler had shown him into Mr. Gardiner's study where they sipped an exquisite French brandy while they awaited the ladies, who had yet to make their appearance. The elder children returned from a quick walk with their nursemaid but were soon ushered upstairs with haste for their tea, leaving the two gentlemen alone to savour their spirits.

"I must thank you for arranging this evening for us," said Mr. Gardiner. "My nieces have been quite anticipating a night at the theatre and the opportunity to wear one of their new gowns."

The firelight reflected in his glass while he took a breath in a futile attempt to settle himself. "I am pleased all of you can join me. I take my sister to the theatre on occasion, but being in such a public place makes her uneasy, so I do not force her to go often." He cleared his throat. "My sister enjoyed her tea with Miss Bennet and Miss Elizabeth immensely. Thank you for allowing them to come." While he adored hearing Georgiana giggle and talk as she had, he had to bemoan the wall that separated him from his sister and Miss Elizabeth. What he would not have given to be allowed in the music room! How frustrating to be so close, yet so far. How could he prove to Elizabeth he was not an ogre if he never spoke to her?

"The girls enjoyed themselves; I assure you. Lizzy spoke of how impressed she is with Miss Darcy. She said your sister is quite accomplished."

"Georgiana practices as often as she can. From the moment my mother helped her first press the keys, she wanted nothing more than to play." He blinked in a rapid fashion at the memory of his mother sitting at the pianoforte with a young Georgiana in her lap. She had never recovered fully after his sister's birth, yet had never let her fragile state interfere with spending time with her children.

"Your sister must cherish the memory."

"She was too young to remember when my mother first introduced her to the instrument, but she has other memories. I assure you; they are treasured."

At a knock upon the door, they both turned as Mrs. Gardiner entered. "Jane and I are in the hall. Lizzy was fetching her gloves and will join us in a moment. I hope we are not late."

"No, not at all." Darcy drank the last swallow of his brandy and set the glass on the tray while Mr. Gardiner did the same. When he and Mr. Gardiner stepped into the hall, he looked upward to the stairs in time for Miss Elizabeth to appear and almost choked on a swift inhale of breath. She was stunning. The ruby silk creation she wore boasted of a sheer white overlay on the skirt with tiny ribbon roses trimming the waist and the top edge of her bodice. Rose embroidery embellished the white sleeves and finished the ensemble well. A necklace of ruby-coloured beads wrapped around her neck, standing out against the paler flesh of her throat.

"Good evening, Mr. Darcy," she said when she reached the bottom.

He gulped and clenched his hands at his sides lest he touch her. "Miss Elizabeth, I am pleased you and your family could join me. May I say how lovely you are? Miss Bennet, Mrs. Gardiner, you are looking well tonight too." While he spoke, Miss Elizabeth lifted an eyebrow with a matching curve to one side of her lips.

Miss Bennet and Mrs. Gardiner spoke, but he could not have repeated what they said since once his eyes returned to Miss Elizabeth, all else faded away. He held out his arm. "Miss Elizabeth, may I escort you to the carriage?"

Her tongue peeked out and moistened her lips, forcing him to resist drawing closer to her. How he wanted to claim those lips, yet she would surely slap him if he made the attempt. Was she trying to kill him with the temptation? She glanced past him to her aunt, but nodded. As soon as a maid helped her don her cape, she stepped beside him and rested her hand upon his sleeve. "Shall we, Mr. Darcy?"

Once they were inside the equipage, their party chatted during the ride to Drury Lane, though Miss Elizabeth, who sat across from him, was quiet. Was she uncomfortable with his presence? Had she not wished to see Hamlet? She had taken no more than a peek at him before she took his arm. What if she never gave him the opportunity to win her heart? His mind would not settle. He had too many questions that he could not answer.

He shook off the dark mood threatening to ruin his evening. The last time he was in such a state, he had made that ridiculous comment about Miss Elizabeth at the assembly. He could not behave so again. He would ruin whatever slim chance he had to make her his. That would simply not do.

When they arrived, he and Mr. Gardiner alighted first. Mr. Gardiner stepped up to the door and helped his wife and

Miss Bennet, then guided them towards the entrance while Miss Elizabeth stepped down with his aid. "Thank you, sir."

Her hand on his arm lightened his heart. With her so close, he took the opportunity to catch a glimpse of her out of the corner of his eye. She looked down, which gave him a perfect view of the side of her head, her ebony curls peeking from the hood of her pearl-coloured cape.

His footmen, who had rushed inside before them, assisted in the removal of their coats before they hastened to his box ahead of their party. Without the impediment of the cape, his eyes traced over the ruby silk bandeau that threaded through her locks. She took his breath away.

"Forgive me!" At a slap to his shoulder, he turned to meet his cousin's cheerful visage. "I could not get away in time to accompany you to Cheapside, but at least I shall not miss the performance." Richard bowed over Miss Elizabeth's hand. "Miss Elizabeth," he said with a grin before greeting the Gardiners and Miss Bennet.

"Will Miss Darcy not be joining us?"

His heart sped up until it could have burst from his chest. Miss Elizabeth spoke to him—not just spoke to him, but initiated a conversation. "As you know, she is shy, and after a difficult summer, has preferred not to appear in public. Other than her piano master, my aunt, and her companion, she does not enjoy the society of many people. She has expressed no desire to attend the theatre or even attend a musical performance of late."

"I am sorry to hear the summer was such a trial for her. She is a dear, sweet girl. I greatly enjoyed my time with her on Wednesday."

"As she did with you," he said. "She mentioned joining us for supper, so you will have the opportunity to speak to her then." He motioned to Mr. Gardiner, and at the man's nod, they pushed through the crowd towards the stairs. Meanwhile, his mind turned and turned. He was pleased, of course, that Miss Elizabeth enjoyed the company of his sister, but what if they became great friends and Miss Elizabeth never warmed to him? What a torture that would be!

"I appreciate your kindness to Georgiana. She has never had many friends. I fear the estates near Pemberley have a number of young boys, so she has been forced to endure the company of a much older brother instead."

She tipped her head to look up at him with a soft smile. "She claims you are the best of brothers, so I do not believe she has suffered. You have raised her well."

With a shake of his head, he sighed. "Not so very well. I fear I have failed her more than once."

"No parent is perfect, sir. I am certain you did the best you could."

"Thank you," he said. Their gazes held for a bit before her cheeks pinked in a becoming manner, and she diverted her eyes.

As they made their way, no one of his particular acquaintance drew his notice. An unusual occurrence, but he would not object to the lack of unwanted attention. Miss Elizabeth shifted away from him once they were inside the box, and his arm appeared empty without her delicate hand perched atop the wool of his topcoat. The Gardiners, Miss Bennet, and his cousin stepped over to the chairs while he followed Miss Elizabeth to the edge of the balcony.

Her gaze roved over the stage and the seats below them while a few people looked up at them from the gallery. The features of a few were familiar, but she was not acquainted with them. "Is that Mr. Bingley?"

His eyes followed the path of hers until they landed upon the occupants of a box across the theatre. Charles Bingley's ginger-blond hair stood out as did that of Miss Bingley's. "I believe it is." Blast! If Miss Bingley noticed him, she would insist upon greeting him. She was the last person with whom he wished to endure this evening.

Miss Elizabeth scraped her teeth along her bottom lip and peered up at him. "May I ask a rather intrusive question without causing offence?"

He frowned and clasped his hands behind his back. "You may ask whatever you wish to know."

She glanced over to her sister then back to him. "When you and Mr. Bingley departed Netherfield, Miss Bingley sent a letter to Jane, in which she hinted that Mr. Bingley is soon to be betrothed to Georgiana." Before he could respond, she held up a hand. "I thought her to be misleading Jane at the time, and now that I know your sister, I find the match all the more unlikely."

He clenched his teeth and released them. Of all the suppositions for Miss Bingley to make. "My sister is far too young to be betrothed, and when she is considered an appropriate age, she will decide when she will come out as well as who she will wed. She and Bingley are acquainted, but their affection is more that of a brother and sister." He peered over his shoulder to Miss Bennet. "I hope your sister was not dismayed by Miss Bingley's claims."

"She was indeed," said Miss Elizabeth. "Though their acquaintance was brief, my sister came to have a high regard for the gentleman. She thought him all a young man should be."

If Darcy could have closed his eyes and scolded himself, he would have. Miss Bennet's demeanour had always been modest, but what if she possessed a reserved disposition similar to his? She would have never revealed her most intimate feelings before all of Meryton. "I am grieved to hear it. I was unaware her heart had been touched."

Her lips were pressed into a flat line. "Mr. Bingley gave every impression he was attached to her. He seemed so open and amiable. She accepted his attentions as sincere."

Darcy peered across the theatre. "I doubt Bingley knows of the letter or what his sister has said." He turned back to Miss Elizabeth to better gauge her feelings on the matter. "If he were to come to Gracechurch Street, do you think she would accept his call?"

"I cannot say. She and my aunt visited Miss Bingley and Mrs. Hurst, but when those ladies returned the call, they behaved in a cold and rude manner. Poor Jane—she had believed them to be friends. She was devastated."

He nodded and peered back across the theatre, only to be met with the eyes of Bingley, as well as his sister upon them. The curtain upon the stage opened so he held out an arm. "We should take our seats."

When they made to sit, two chairs remained that were side-by-side in front of the Gardiners. How was he to endure an entire performance so close to her? The light rose scent of her perfume pulled at him, urging him closer until he could touch his nose to her flesh and inhale her essence along with the heady floral scent.

Her hand rested upon her leg, and how he itched to take it in his, remove her glove, and touch the softness of her skin with the tips of his fingers. He took in a deep breath and slowly released it. Patience! In order to open her heart to him, he required patience. He was so consumed by Miss Elizabeth's proximity that his thoughts centred on her and her expressions at the events of the play. He remained thus until he jolted from his reverie at her laugh.

"Mr. Darcy, are you well?"

He could not but smile in return. "Yes, forgive me. I am afraid I was wool-gathering."

"I sent James and Peter for wine," said Richard. His cousin clapped him on the shoulder and leaned down next to his ear. "James indicated Bingley is in the passage. He arrived just before the interval."

Darcy blinked and glanced about him. How had the interval come so soon? "Forgive me, Miss Elizabeth, but I must speak to Bingley. If he asks of your sister, what would you have me tell him?"

Her eyes widened and she took a quick peek at Miss Bennet, who spoke to her aunt and uncle. "I am unsure. I do not believe she expects him to renew his addresses."

Richard stood along with them. "I imagine he will want to join our party."

Darcy pressed his lips together. "I must go to him, else he will insist upon entering the box. I would not want him to disturb your sister in front of so many people." She nodded, so he stepped around her and into the corridor.

"Darcy!" Bingley hastened closer and glanced at the door behind Darcy. "I never expected to see you here this evening, and with the Miss Bennets! I had no idea they were even in London."

"I believe they arrived a se'nnight ago. My cousin introduced me to their uncle, and we dined at their home in Cheapside a few days ago."

His friend raked a hand through his hair. "I am astounded that you would invite them to the theatre."

Darcy flinched back a bit. "Why? Because Mr. Gardiner is a wealthy tradesman? I have attended the theatre with you and your sisters. You are not so dissimilar, are you?" While Miss Bingley oft times commented on the Bennet family's connection to trade, she could have been more severe upon her own ties.

Bingley started and barked out an odd sort of laugh. "I suppose you are correct." He rubbed his hands together. "Do you think Miss Bennet would accept my call? I had intended to return to Netherfield until Caroline and Louisa followed us to town. I have regretted the way in which I departed. I never took my leave or assured her of my return." He brightened. "I could join your party for the rest of the performance."

Darcy set his hand upon Bingley's shoulder. "I do not believe that is possible. I learnt this evening that Miss Bingley penned a letter to Miss Bennet, informing her you were to soon become betrothed to Georgiana."

His friend gasped and paled. "I mean no disrespect to your sister, but I would never."

"I know," said Darcy, "but Miss Bennet could do no more than believe your sister's claims. I am concerned the theatre would not be a prudent place to become reacquainted. You do not want to become the performance."

Bingley winced and shook his head. "I had not considered—"

"Instead, you could join us for a light supper after the play?" Bingley opened his mouth, but Darcy held up a finger. "But, if you are to come, your sisters are not welcome. After what has occurred, I shall not have them upsetting my guests with their snide comments and veiled insults."

After nodding vigorously, Bingley grasped his hand and began shaking it. "Thank you! I shall accompany them home, then claim fatigue and sneak out."

All of Darcy's forbearance was required not to roll his eyes. When would his friend heed his own heart and mind instead of the opinions and manipulations of those around him? "Bingley, one day, you must stand up to your sisters, lest they dictate your life—including whom you marry. I can assure you, even Miss Bennet may not tolerate your sisters after their correspondence."

"Mr. Darcy! There you are!"

His stomach sank like a rock when Miss Bingley reached up and waved from further down the corridor. "You must return to your seats and take your sister with you. She will not be admitted to my box. I will not tolerate her cloying behaviour in front of my guests."

"Of course," said Bingley. "Thank you, Darcy." His ginger-blond hair bobbed through the crowd, but he did not wait to be assured Bingley had escorted his sister away from them and ducked back into the box.

As soon as he stepped inside, Miss Elizabeth hurried over to him. "Well?"

"He is to come to supper this evening. I thought it a better solution than him calling at Gracechurch Street. If your sister decides she has no desire to receive his calls, he will not know where your aunt and uncle live. His sisters know, but I doubt either would tell him." He prayed she would agree with him.

She glanced over to Miss Bennet before her gaze met his. "I agree. I just do not know when to warn her."

"He will need to escort his sisters home to Grosvenor Square first. You will have an opportunity when we arrive at Darcy House."

Miss Elizabeth smiled at him. "You have thought of everything."

She had smiled at him. What he would not give to have her do so again and again!

Chapter 6

As soon as the play concluded, Elizabeth rose and tugged Jane into the far corner of the box. "Have you noticed Mr. Bingley across the theatre?"

Jane tried to look around her. "What? Mr. Bingley is here?"

"He saw us before the play began and spoke to Mr. Darcy during the interval."

"Why did Mr. Darcy not bring him to greet us?" Her shoulders sank and her expression fell. "Or did Mr. Bingley have no wish—"

"No, Mr. Bingley did enquire of you." Elizabeth took her sister's hands and squeezed. "After the manner in which Mr. Bingley departed Netherfield, Mr. Darcy requested his friend wait until after the performance. He was concerned Mr. Bingley may upset you."

After she blinked a few times, Jane frowned. "Have you spoken to Mr. Darcy of my disappointment?"

"Since making Georgiana's acquaintance, I asked him of Miss Bingley's claim of a coming betrothal between Mr. Bingley and his sister, which Mr. Darcy refuted. Tonight, when he learnt Mr. Bingley was in the corridor, he had concerns after Miss Bingley's and Mrs. Hurst's treatment of you. He questioned whether you would still desire to continue an acquaintance with the brother." She squeezed Jane's hands. "The gentleman, however, was adamant about speaking to you, so Mr. Darcy offered for Mr. Bingley to join us for supper at his home tonight."

"Oh!"

Elizabeth glanced over her shoulder. Her aunt and uncle conversed with Mr. Darcy and the colonel. Her gaze locked with Mr. Darcy's and he lifted his eyebrows. Would she have ever considered he would be of such aid to them—that she would conspire with him?

When she once again faced Jane, her sister stared down at their hands. "Dearest? I hope Mr. Darcy did not overstep? He thought if you never wished to see Mr. Bingley after tonight, Mr. Bingley would not know where to find us in Cheapside. He could not call should you not wish for his presence."

"Is it terrible that I do not know what I want?"

Her sister's pained expression tore at her. "Of course not, but perhaps during supper, you may understand what you desire for the future. Just do not consider Mama in your decision. She need not live with Mr. Bingley for the rest of her life if you accept him."

Jane kissed Elizabeth on the cheek. "I do believe Mama would move into Netherfield without delay if she could, but thank you, Lizzy." She peered over Elizabeth's shoulder. "And do thank Mr. Darcy for me. His consideration of my feelings does him credit."

"I agree," said Elizabeth. He had arranged this interaction with Mr. Bingley with sensitivity and compassion. Who was this man? A hand between Elizabeth's shoulder blades made her give a slight jump.

"I believe we should be departing." Her aunt glanced between them. "Is aught amiss?"

"No," said Jane, shaking her head. "Lizzy was warning me that Mr. Bingley is to be at supper. She and Mr. Darcy did not want me caught unawares."

"So, we will make the acquaintance of this capricious young man, it seems." Aunt Gardiner pressed them towards the door. "I must say that I do hope he leaves his sisters at home."

Jane gasped. "Aunt!"

Uncle Gardiner offered his arm to his wife while the colonel escorted Jane, leaving Elizabeth to accept Mr. Darcy's elbow. "Is your sister well?"

"Yes. She is confused, but I believe I would feel the same were I in her predicament." He looked down at her and her heartbeat quickened. Gooseflesh prickled at the back of her neck. The continued connection between them unsettled her so she diverted her gaze back to the room before her.

"Mr. Darcy!" Was that Miss Bingley's head bouncing above the crowd?

"Pray, pretend you have not seen her," he said, leaning a bit closer to her. "My driver will have the carriage near the entrance. We do not have much further."

She bit her cheek to keep from laughing. "Mr. Darcy, I am appalled. Do you not want to speak to the lady?" She tried as best she could to sound shocked while he hurried them through the crowd. Hopefully, he understood her teasing.

"Lord, no. I have enjoyed this evening immensely. I tolerate Miss Bingley due to my friendship with the lady's brother. If not for Bingley, I would have given her the cut direct ages ago." He ducked them around a man of considerable height and girth, though not so much as to hide either of them fully. "I have never provided her any encouragement, yet she sinks her talons into my arms as a falcon would its prey."

She covered her mouth with her free hand and laughed. Why had Mr. Darcy behaved so differently in Hertfordshire? Had Mr. Darcy abandoned his sense of humour in London?

The cold air was a shock when he tugged her through the door. She looked over her shoulder. Where was the footman? "My cape!"

His forehead was creased when he turned. "Forgive me. I could think of nothing more than escaping Miss Bingley. You must think me horrid." He looked in one direction then the other. "Where is that carriage?" At a call, he spun around. "There! Make haste!" As soon as he handed her inside, he pulled two rugs from underneath the opposite seat so she could protect herself from the chill, but he did not join her inside the equipage.

"Are you not cold, sir?"

He rubbed his hands together as he exhaled in a puff of white in front of him. "I am warm enough, thank you. I do wonder what has kept the remainder of our party."

She slid across the seat, so she was next to the door. "My uncle may have been stopped by an acquaintance."

When next their eyes met, he drew closer and leaned against the opening. "Are you warmer?"

"Yes, thank you." What was wrong with her voice? Why could she not speak louder than a near whisper?

He cleared his throat. "Miss Elizabeth, while we have this moment, I must beg your forgiveness for some unfortunate words I said while in Hertfordshire."

She stared at him. He desired her forgiveness? She arched her eyebrow. "I am certain I could forgive you. Are you requesting forgiveness for a particular event or for the entirety of our acquaintance in that county?"

His lips curved ever-so-slightly. "You may recall what I said of Georgiana's summer."

"Of course," she said.

"During the autumn, my aunt Lady Fitzwilliam took Georgiana and ensured she was well. Frustrated I could do naught to be of aid to my sister, I joined Bingley at Netherfield. I am not comfortable around those with whom I am not particularly acquainted and attempted to remain behind from the assembly, but Bingley would not have it."

"Ah, you are referring to saying I am 'merely tolerable.'"

He nodded, and watched his hands, his brow furrowed. "I could make a multitude of excuses: I am uncomfortable with people I do not know well, I despised being away from Georgiana, I did not care for the gossip of my supposed income circulating the room." He sighed. "Regardless of the reasons, I should not have been so disagreeable and rude."

"I am sorry you were experiencing such a trying time," she said. "I am happy to provide whatever absolution you seek."

His head lifted and the gaze of his brilliant blue eyes captured her. "You must know I have come to regret those words. I have never found you merely tolerable."

"You have not?" Why had her voice begun to sound so odd again?

"I have long thought you one of the most handsome ladies of my acquaintance."

Her heart pounded in her ears as his fingers lifted and grazed along her jawline. She could not breathe. She could not move. She may as well have been as frozen as a block of ice.

"There you are!"

Mr. Darcy's hand recoiled, and he stepped back.

"Forgive us the delay. Miss Bingley caught us while we donned our coats." The colonel wore a wide grin as he approached, laughing as he drew closer. "She said you did not seem to hear her. I told her I did not know where you had disappeared, which was the truth."

"Lizzy," said Jane as she climbed inside. "You must have been freezing without this." She handed her the cape.

While Elizabeth wrapped the garment around her shoulders, she shook her head. "Mr. Darcy ushered me into the carriage without delay and provided these rugs. I was not cold for long."

Aunt Gardiner sat beside her and took her hand. "Are you well?"

"Yes, Aunt. Mr. Darcy hurried to avoid speaking to Miss Bingley."

Her uncle, the colonel, and Mr. Darcy situated themselves across from the ladies as her aunt rolled her eyes. "I do not blame Mr. Darcy after that woman's call to Gracechurch Street. A more ill-mannered person I have yet to meet."

During the journey to Mr. Darcy's home, the occupants of the carriage, other than she and Mr. Darcy, discussed the performance as well as the play, but Elizabeth could not remove her eyes from the shadow of Mr. Darcy across from her. He begged her forgiveness for saying she was tolerable. He thought her the handsomest lady of his acquaintance. He had asked to introduce her to his sister. Could he be meaning to—? No! He was the nephew of an earl and master of a great estate. He was destined for someone with connections and a sizeable fortune. Not poor Lizzy Bennet of Longbourn, who would inherit a measly thousand pounds upon the death of her mother.

When the vehicle came to an abrupt stop, she gazed through the window at the large stone house before her, its light spilling from the windows and the front door as it opened. The step was placed, and she bent closer to the glass while she waited to alight. Her unease was as pronounced tonight as it was a few days ago when she first set eyes upon his Park Lane home. She was certain, if attempted, one could fit Longbourn inside the outer walls of this house without difficulty.

Mr. Darcy helped her to the pavement where she looked up, then turned in a circle, peering at the darkened trees of the park across the street. "Have you ever been to Hyde Park?"

"Yes, my aunt likes to take the children to the Serpentine in the spring." When she faced the house once more, she swallowed hard and gaped until his elbow appeared before her.

"May I?"

She could do no more than nod as he led her up the stairs and inside. Once her cape was removed and hastened away, she lifted her head to the *trompe l'oeil* and gold filigree along the ceiling, just as she had during her first call.

"My father saw a ceiling like it in Tuscany during his Grand Tour. When he became master, he hired an Italian artist to create the effect."

"'Tis lovely."

"Lizzy!" Elizabeth pressed her hand to her chest as Georgiana bounced in front of her, an enormous smile upon her face.

"Poppet, you gave Miss Elizabeth a fright, crying her name in such a fashion," said Colonel Fitzwilliam. "Perhaps next time, not quite so loud."

"I am sorry," said the young lady. "I have been waiting all night for you to arrive. I tried reading, but I could scarce understand the words. My mind was too preoccupied knowing you would soon come."

Elizabeth could only smile at her enthusiasm. She was a dear, sweet girl. "I am flattered. I do hope you will play for us tonight."

"Oh, yes, you must!" Jane's hands were pressed together in front of her.

Miss Darcy perked up and brought her shoulder up to her chin. "Perhaps I shall."

"What have you done to Georgiana?" asked the colonel. "I do not believe I have ever witnessed her so at ease with someone who is not family."

Her aunt and uncle stood beside Mr. Darcy, who held out his arm towards a door. "Why do we not go to the drawing room while we await the meal?"

Georgiana looped her arm through Elizabeth's and tugged her through the entry until they were seated upon the sofa. "You must tell me all about the play. Did you see anyone of our acquaintance? Was the performance enjoyable?"

Mr. Darcy laughed, a low rich sound that sent a shiver down to Elizabeth's toes. "Georgie, if you wanted to know so much about the theatre, you should have joined us. I am certain Miss Bennet and Miss Elizabeth would have welcomed your company. You are well aware Richard and I would have been pleased for you to have attended."

"Of course, we would," said Jane.

The young lady dismissed her brother's comment with a wave of her hand. "I did not want to go. I just remember Lizzy is not fond of tragedies, so I wished to know if she was entertained."

"I was excessively diverted." Elizabeth picked up a book from the side table. "Who is reading Shelley?" She held the book before Georgiana. "Is this yours?"

"Oh, that is Fitzwilliam's."

Mr. Darcy stepped forward. "I apologise. I was reading that before I departed for Cheapside. I shall have a servant put it away."

"No," said Elizabeth. "I am not bothered. What do you think of it? I have heard of *The Devil's Walk,* but my father has been thus far unable to procure a copy."

His hand returned to rest at his side. "I have found it well done. If you would care to read it, I would be pleased to lend it to you once I am finished. I should reach the end by tomorrow and would be happy to call at Gracechurch Street." His eyes bored into her. Why did he seem to be seeking permission for more than the loan of a book?

Georgiana gasped. "Brother, you should show Lizzy the library. She may find a book to borrow until you are finished with the Shelley."

Elizabeth returned the book to the table with care. "I appreciate the offer, Georgiana, but my uncle does have a library to keep me entertained. Do not feel you must atone for reading your own book." Why was tonight so different from a mere few days ago? She had not been so ill at ease in the company of just Georgiana and Jane.

"Mr. Gardiner, would you mind if I showed Miss Elizabeth the library?"

Her head shot up at Mr. Darcy's request. "Pray, 'tis not necessary."

With a lift of his bushy eyebrows, her uncle looked back and forth between them. "I see no harm in looking, Lizzy. You have read most of my collection by now unless you want to read them all over again." He tipped his head down a bit. "I do ask that the door remain open."

"Of course," said Mr. Darcy.

She stood and made to open her mouth, but a slight push to her back made her turn. Had Georgiana given her a shove? Both Georgiana and Jane motioned for her to go, so she followed him into the hall where he waited for her to join him.

"I do not wish to impose."

He smiled and offered his arm. "You are no imposition. The library is one of my favourite rooms. I am happy to show it to you."

As soon as they entered, her eyes surely bulged from their sockets at the size of the room, not to mention the number of books lining the shelves. If this was his London home, how extensive was the library at Pemberley?

A landscape above the mantel drew her attention, and she stepped before it. A grand house stood proud and tall at the base of a wooded peak, a river winding across the pastureland before it. "Is this your home?"

"Yes, that is Pemberley during my grandfather's time. Not much has changed, but perhaps the rose garden my mother added, as well as the cascade. What do you think? Do you approve?"

She glanced at him over her shoulder. "I believe there are few who would not approve."

"But I do not seek their opinion. I fear I care only for yours." The butterflies in her stomach took flight, circling wider and wider, while her breathing quickened. He stood straight with one leg slightly kicked out to one side. She had never denied how handsome he was, but when he spoke in such a way and in that low tone, she lost control over her own body. The flutterings and her heart beating in a heavy cadence against her ribs were not a usual occurrence. What was happening to her?

"Mine?" Good Lord! Now, she could not speak in more than a monosyllable.

That hammering in her chest increased as he stepped closer. "I know I have done little to garner your good opinion, but I hope to improve my character in your eyes. As much as I would like you to consent to a courtship—"

"Yes." She started and clutched at her stomach. Had she just agreed to a courtship with Mr. Darcy?

His eyes had flared before the beginnings of a smile peeked from his cheeks. "Did you say yes?"

Had she? She swallowed and struggled to breathe. She could not faint!

"Elizabeth," he said, stepping forward and grabbing her arms. "Are you well?"

"I do not know. I am light-headed."

He ushered her to a chair and poured what appeared to be brandy. "Take small sips." After he pressed the glass into her hand, he knelt before her. "I intended to request your permission to call. If you wish to know me better before you consent to more, I shall not complain."

Her eyes searched his. "Are you certain you desire a courtship with me?" Could she marry him? For the entirety of their acquaintance, she had vilified Mr. Darcy and accused him of ill-doing. After all, she had Mr. Wickham's hardships to lay at his feet, but how to reconcile that man's description of Georgiana with the living, breathing girl who practically trembled in fear at speaking to a new acquaintance? How could she believe Mr. Wickham when he spoke of such an innocent creature in such a way?

Then, what of Mr. Darcy's behaviour since she happened upon him in her uncle's shop? He had been agreeable and solicitous of not only her but also her sister. She rather liked this Mr. Darcy as opposed to the one she met in Hertfordshire.

"Miss Elizabeth?"

"Yes, I think I do." His barely perceptible smile grew, and gooseflesh spread up her arms and across her shoulders. Thank goodness she was wearing gloves, so he could not tell.

"You think?"

As much as the idea of courting him terrified her, she could not deny how he drew her notice and unsettled her more than any man she had ever known. She took in a fortifying breath. "Yes, my answer is yes." Her voice all but disappeared again, but he had heard. His wide grin would have told everyone in the room if they had been in company.

"Mr. Darcy," said a voice from behind her. "Mr. Bingley has arrived."

His shoulders dropped. "As much as I would like to remain here with you for the rest of the evening, we should return. I do not want your uncle challenging me on the most memorable night of my life."

She took his proffered arm. "The most memorable night of your life?"

He looked down upon her with a lop-sided smile so bright, it could have lit all of Hyde Park. "The most memorable night of my life thus far, of course. The only thing that could improve upon this evening would be your acceptance of my hand."

Her palm once again found her stomach. Would these butterflies be her constant companions, or would she ever become accustomed to this new Mr. Darcy?

Chapter 7

After a leisurely meal, the gentlemen stood while Georgiana led the ladies to the music room for tea, with Richard hopping from his seat to escort Miss Bennet. No doubt, the rich notes of the pianoforte would be filtering through the hall before long, and how Darcy longed to hear that rich melody along with the laughter of his sister with Miss Elizabeth!

Richard made a swift return as Darcy stood. "Shall we adjourn to my study?"

"By all means, yes," said Richard. While Bingley was as cheerful and talkative as he ever was during the meal, Richard watched him with gritted teeth. His cousin had never taken to Bingley, but he would never cause a scene in front of the ladies. In light of Bingley's presence, Richard was certain to desire a substantial glass of brandy. Darcy also did not doubt that Richard escorted Miss Bennet in an effort to unnerve Bingley.

As they made to depart the dining room, his cousin grabbed him by the elbow and held him back while Mr. Gardiner and Bingley stepped into the hall. "The pup is watching your marked attention to Miss Elizabeth. I cannot be certain, but at times, he appears annoyed by it."

"I cannot understand why, unless he harbours some resentment about Miss Bennet. The predicament with that lady is his own fault as well as that of his sisters. If he truly had feelings for her, he should not have required the opinions of all and sundry to pursue her."

Richard laughed and shook his head. "Yet, you turned surly and unsociable when you attempted to persuade yourself against Miss Elizabeth."

"You can be a right arse, Cousin."

"So can you, Cousin."

He could not leave his guests waiting, so he forged ahead, leading the gentlemen into his study where he invited everyone to sit. Richard took his usual chair by the fire while Mr. Gardiner and Bingley sat on opposite ends of the sofa.

"I must say, 'tis a pleasure to finally make your acquaintance, Mr. Gardiner," said Bingley as he accepted a glass of brandy. "Your nieces speak highly of you, sir."

Mr. Gardiner smiled in a way that did not reach his eyes. "I am pleased they think well of me. I enjoy their society when my brother allows them to visit. They have become kind and generous ladies. I could not be more proud of them. They are quite dear to both me and my wife."

Darcy sat in the chair opposite Richard. "Georgiana has taken great pleasure in their company, and Miss Bennet and Miss Elizabeth have done well to put my reticent sister at ease."

"A feat not easily accomplished," said Richard.

After clearing his throat, Bingley shifted in his seat. "Mr. Gardiner, I wish to call upon Miss Bennet and hope you would be agreeable. I desire to continue our acquaintance from Hertfordshire."

The bushy eyebrows of Mr. Gardiner drew down a bit in the centre. "Have you made this request of my niece?"

"Not as yet. I thought to secure your approval first."

"Well," said Mr. Gardiner in a drawn out manner. "I am loath to give my permission when you have not secured her agreement. If you apply to Jane and she agrees, we shall speak further, but no sooner."

Bingley reddened a bit and jerked his gaze to his glass. "Of course, sir. I understand. I shall be certain to apply to her once we re-join the ladies."

They sipped their drinks in silence for but a moment before Bingley laughed. "I say, Darcy, my sister was quite put out that you disappeared into the crush at the theatre. She fussed and fumed and insisted you had a lady on your arm, which I assured her could not be possible." Richard snickered into his glass, making Bingley frown in his direction.

Darcy's back stiffened. "I was escorting Miss Elizabeth to my carriage. We were somehow separated from the Gardiners in the crowd, so I rushed us outside to await the rest of our party." Again, his cousin practically tittered. When had he become such a woman?

"Caroline was also exceedingly curious about where I was going. She will be furious that I left her behind."

"Why tell her?" said Richard. "Do you tell her aught that you do?"

"No!" Bingley straightened and sputtered his response. "Do not be preposterous!"

"I do not see how it is preposterous. I would not be surprised if you required your sister's instruction on how to fasten your breeches."

Darcy gasped. "Richard!" Mr. Gardiner pressed his lips together and dropped his gaze to his lap, his shoulders giving an occasional twitch.

Meanwhile, Bingley shot from his seat. "I shall not be treated thus."

A sigh escaped Darcy's lips before he could stop it. "Perhaps we should return to the ladies."

His cousin rose and lifted his glass. "A capital idea. I am certain Miss Bennet is desirous of a gentleman's company after suffering Bingley's during the meal."

Darcy's hand clapped down on his friend's shoulder before the younger man could retort while Mr. Gardiner and Richard departed and made their way towards the dulcet tones of the pianoforte. "Why do you let him bait you?"

"Why do you allow it?"

"I have asked that he not do so, yet you have a habit of putting the opinions of others' before your own and allowing your sister to influence your decisions. If you want to earn the respect of Richard and others, you need to prove you are your own man—you answer to no one."

His friend laughed in a manner Darcy had never heard before. "What of you?"

"What of me?"

"You demeaned the Bennets and said Miss Elizabeth was 'tolerable but not handsome enough to tempt you,' yet now you invite the family to the theatre and your home for dinner." Bingley's eyes flared. "You are courting her!"

Darcy's head jerked back. "I have no interest in Miss Bennet."

"No! Miss Elizabeth! Caroline was jealous of Miss Elizabeth and often singled her out, particularly in your company," said Bingley, wagging his finger. "I never understood until now. She perceived your interest in Miss Elizabeth. She will be none too pleased."

"I could not care less of how your sister feels, Bingley. I made the decision to pursue Miss Elizabeth, and I shall not be swayed from it—not by you, not by your sisters, and not by anyone else."

"Without a fortune, she will be a laughingstock."

"Yet you wish to call upon Miss Bennet," said Darcy. "Do you intend to court her or are you to abandon her once again? Your sister does not approve of the match. Will she influence your decision? I may have been reluctant to court Miss Elizabeth at one time, but I decided to follow my heart, and no one will persuade me to walk away from Miss Elizabeth. Are you committed to Miss Bennet in the same manner? If not, do not injure the lady any more than you already have."

"But you told me—"

"I told you I saw no hint of regard, but I do not know the lady well. She could have displayed her feelings to you without my noticing. If you truly desired her as your wife, why would my words give you cause to abandon hope? I would not permit my cousin's, or aunt's, or uncle's persuasions to deter me from Miss Elizabeth—only she can force me to quit my pursuit." He let out a swift exhale. "If you will pardon me, I should like to return to her. Pray, consider Miss Bennet and her feelings in your decision. She was hurt when you left Hertfordshire. She may not wish to try again, but you will have to ask her for yourself."

He held out an arm to a wide-eyed and lax-jawed Bingley, who clamped his mouth shut and walked in a stiff manner through the hall. When they entered the music room, Richard sat with Mrs. Gardiner and Miss Bennet while they watched Georgiana perform. With swift steps, Darcy sat beside Miss Elizabeth, who smiled at him before her attention returned to his sister. He dearly loved when she smiled at him! When the sonatina ended, Miss Bennet approached Georgiana, and the pair began flipping through the music.

"The gentlemen returned with a swiftness I was not expecting."

He turned some to face Miss Elizabeth. How he wished he could draw closer! "My cousin and Bingley do not get on well. I thought it best to join the rest of the party before they had too much time to interact."

Her eyes searched his expression. "I feel there is more to the story than you are saying. Perhaps one day you will reveal it to me?"

"When we are not in company, I shall gladly tell you as much as I can." And he would. There was little he would deny her if it was in his power to give.

"Lizzy, Georgiana has selected that piece you sang a few days ago. Your voice sounded so lovely with Georgiana's skilful execution of the accompaniment. I am certain Aunt and Uncle would love to hear it."

"Yes, we would," said Mrs. Gardiner. Darcy could only agree with Mrs. Gardiner. Few things gave him as much pleasure as Miss Elizabeth's voice, as well as the emotion of her performances on the pianoforte.

Miss Elizabeth let out an exhale and stood. "I suppose I shall have no peace until I surrender, so very well, I shall sing."

As Miss Bennet had said, Georgiana played the piece to perfection, which was only complemented by Miss Elizabeth's lilting voice. Her pronunciation of the Italian phrasing was not flawless, but her interpretation did not disappoint. He could do no more than stare in rapt attention while she sang.

Just before the end of the aria, Miss Bennet crossed the room, returning to her aunt's side. Bingley wore a frown as he watched her, his displeasure deepening as the lady seemed to ignore his attempts to catch her eye. Had he requested to call upon her? If not, what could he have said to cause such an uncharacteristic response in the lady?

After two more songs, the Gardiners called for their carriage and thanked Darcy for a splendid evening. He took the liberty of holding Miss Elizabeth's hand a bit longer than was proper when he handed her into the carriage, but she did not seem to object. Instead, she bestowed a beatific smile upon him before the equipage pulled away from the kerb and into the night.

"How did Miss Bennet respond to your request?" he asked Bingley as soon as the carriage was out of sight.

"I have no desire to speak of it. Thank you for dinner, Darcy. I bid you good night." He gave a curt nod to Richard and said, "Fitzwilliam."

As soon as the door closed behind them, Georgiana excused herself to retire, and Richard accompanied him into his study. "I was standing behind where Bingley was attempting to gain Miss Bennet's acceptance of his calls. From what I heard, she told him three times she would need to think on it. She retreated to her aunt's side when he continued to press."

"How did I miss this?"

His cousin snickered. "You were busy wool-gathering of Miss Elizabeth while she sang. I am not surprised you did not hear Bingley."

"I cannot say I blame her," said Darcy.

"Nor can I." Richard poured himself a glass of brandy and sat in his usual chair. "She is far too good for him, and if they were to marry, that sister of his will make her life a misery. I applaud Mr. Gardiner for not giving his permission without his niece's say. His decision does him credit."

"I agree. After meeting his sister, I would not have expected Mr. Gardiner to be a man of such sense and education, but I find I enjoy his company."

Richard grinned and tipped his glass in Darcy's direction. "Though not so much as Miss Elizabeth's."

"Well, no, of course not."

His cousin laughed. "You are lost, Darcy—hopelessly lost."

Chapter 8

Darcy alighted from his carriage, tugged at the bottom of his topcoat and cuffs, then stepped up to the door. After knocking, he inhaled in a futile attempt to calm the nerves usurping control of his body. What was wrong with him? Miss Elizabeth had been amenable to a courtship. It was unlikely she had changed her mind before this morning.

"Good morning, Mr. Darcy." The butler admitted him and took his coat. "The ladies are awaiting you in the drawing room." He stepped over and opened the door. "Mr. Darcy has arrived."

Mrs. Gardiner, Miss Bennet, and Miss Elizabeth all stood when Darcy entered. Once he bowed to their curtseys, he held out a small bouquet of pink roses that proved to be a perfect match to the blush that overspread Miss Elizabeth's cheeks. "I hope you like roses."

"They are lovely." Her careful hands took them from his grip and brought them to her nose. "But where did you find them in December?"

"I have a small hothouse here. I quite surprised the gardener when I bothered him for his aid in stealing a few for your enjoyment. I considered you may have a preference for wildflowers, but 'tis not the season, of course."

"You are fortunate, Mr. Darcy," said Miss Bennet with a soft smile. "I do not believe my sister has ever made the acquaintance of a flower she disliked."

He dipped his chin. "Good morning, Mrs. Gardiner, Miss Bennet. I hope you will forgive me, but the obliging rosebush had only enough blooms for one bouquet."

Mrs. Gardiner resumed her seat and folded her hands in her lap. "Pray, Mr. Darcy, do not be concerned for us. We would never expect you to greet us with flowers and gifts and are content for you to shower them upon Lizzy."

Miss Elizabeth gasped while Miss Bennet laughed. "Aunt!"

He lifted the volume of Shelley. "I also brought you this."

She smiled in a soft way that made him want to take her into his arms and hold her close, but what would she think of his shaking so? He knew nothing of courting a lady, and he had no one to ask. Richard would be useless with such a question, and if he asked Bingley, the addlepate would speak of it in front of Miss Bingley.

"I thank you for bringing this. I shall take good care of it."

When she placed the book on a nearby table, Miss Bennet took the roses. "I shall put these in some water for you."

"Thank you," said Miss Elizabeth.

After clenching and releasing his hands in an attempt to control the slight tremor, he clasped them behind his back. "The weather is a bit warmer today and lacks the sting of the past week."

She glanced out of the window. "Yes, the clouds have allowed the sun to shine. I have enjoyed sitting in the window this morning."

"Would you care for a walk in the park?" He turned to Mrs. Gardiner. "We would not be long."

One side of Mrs. Gardiner's lips curved. "I shall ring the bell for a maid to accompany you. Lizzy, you may want to fetch your pelisse, bonnet, and gloves."

"Yes, of course. If you will pardon me."

"Thank you once again for your invitation to the theatre," said Mrs. Gardiner while she awaited a servant. "We enjoyed the performance as well as the supper at your home. Lizzy and Jane have spoken of the evening often this morning. Their mother and sisters will be quite envious."

"I admit I was pleased with the evening too. I would also like to invite you and your family for dinner on the first evening of Christmastide."

Mrs. Gardiner's smile faltered a bit. "I am afraid we cannot the first evening. We have planned the day with the children. They are so eager for Christmas to arrive, and I cannot disappoint them now."

"No," he said swiftly. "I would never expect you to do so. Perhaps we can arrange for another day during Christmastide?"

"I am certain we would be happy to dine with you again, sir." She pressed her hands together. "If you do not mind the children, we would be pleased to host you and your sister for Christmas. Your cousin is welcome too if he does not plan to pass the day with his parents."

He could not withhold the grin that overspread his face. "I accept your gracious invitation. My sister and I would be quite content to spend the day with your family. Thank you."

"Oh! Pray, pardon me a moment." Mrs. Gardiner bustled over to the entrance to the servants' passage and spoke in hushed tones to the lady in the doorway.

"Have we a chaperone?" asked Miss Elizabeth as she returned with her belongings.

"I am sure we shall soon." He pointed to her dark rose pelisse. "Perhaps we should put on our coats." He struggled to control his hands while he pulled her pelisse from her arm. "May I?"

Her eyes darted to her aunt. "I suppose there is no harm in it."

While the job would usually be relegated to a maid or a footman, he could not resist the opportunity. She slipped her arms in one at a time, but when he drew the garment up to her shoulders, his finger strayed and brushed the base of her neck. Tiny bumps erupted along her shoulders, and she spun around in a swift motion to face him. "Thank you."

He nodded but worked to keep a neutral expression to prevent her embarrassment. She was affected by him! Her fingers worked at the buttons while she watched the fastenings with a renewed vigour. How flushed was her complexion? He picked up her gloves from the arm of the sofa and held them to her.

"Thank you," she said.

When the housekeeper appeared with his great coat and hat, he made quick work of donning them, and soon, they strolled in the direction of the park gates. "Georgiana has spoken of naught but you and Miss Bennet since Saturday. She has expressed a desire to spend more time with you. She enjoys your sister's company but—"

"As I have accepted your courtship, she wishes to spend time with me alone. Pray, do not be concerned with injuring Jane's feelings. She has always possessed a keen sense of understanding. She will not take offence."

"I am relieved to hear it." He stepped up to the kerb and looked for carriages, before leading Miss Elizabeth across. "She asked if you would join her in decorating the house for

Christmas. We could journey to Gracechurch Street in the morning and take you to Darcy House then return you that evening."

She squeezed his arm as she peered up at him. "Pray, tell her I am anticipating the day."

"Would Christmas Eve be agreeable?" He warmed at her willingness to treat Georgiana as not only a good friend, but also a potential sister.

"I have no prior engagements for that day." A light laugh filtered to his ears on the breeze. "If I am to spend the day with your sister, decorating, I feel I must warn you of my clumsy nature."

Clumsy? He had never been witness to any unwieldy or awkward movements on her part. In his eyes, she was grace itself. "Why do you believe yourself so?"

"I do not think, sir. I know without a single doubt. Shall I enumerate the reasons?"

"I am eager to hear them," he said, one side of his lips tugging upward.

Her laugh bubbled a bit louder this time. "Well, when I was ten, I fell from the ladder while picking apples in the orchard. I was thirteen when I fell from Papa's horse and hit my head. If Papa is to be believed, my mother nearly succumbed to an apoplexy when the grooms rushed me into the house."

"Is that why you walk rather than go on horseback to Meryton?"

"I have never banished my fear from the accident, so my father never allowed me to try again."

Darcy glanced over to her dark curls. He was thankful she had not been grievously injured. "Your father is wise. Horses can sense when someone is afraid. Even the most docile of creatures may try to take advantage and cause an injury."

She sighed. "My father said as much himself." She stepped in front of him and turned on her heel to face him. "But you have not let me tell you of all my follies, sir."

"All of your follies?"

That one eyebrow arched in the most alluring way with a crooked smile. "I said I was clumsy. Did you not believe me?"

He laughed in an easy manner. She could pull that sound from him with so little effort. How had he lived these eight and twenty years without her arch manner to tease him from his ill humour? "I would never be so uncharitable."

"You see, the next spring, I tripped in a hole during one of my rambles and broke my ankle. When I was sixteen, I slipped while climbing the shelves in my father's book room—"

"You climbed the shelves of your father's book room?" He surely gaped at her.

"Did you not know? The best books are always at the top."

He chuckled and shook his head. "Was that the last of your escapades?"

"Of course not," she said as she took a step backwards. "At seventeen, I tried climbing the apple tree rather than using the ladder."

"What did you injure?"

"I was fortunate in that I escaped with a few bumps and bruises. My gown, however, proved beyond repair. The dressmaker had just finished it. My mother still chastises me about ruining that gown."

He was charmed. He could listen to her speak thus for days and never be bored. "You are now twenty? What scrape have you found yourself in of late?"

"I have twisted my one ankle twice since then and tripped on the carpet in the parlour." She ticked off each instance on her fingers. "I hurt my wrist breaking the fall, but I do not know if it was broken."

"So, I am to keep you far away from any ladders, horses, and carpets."

She laughed and held her face up to the sun. "I just thought you should be forewarned."

With her eyes closed, he allowed his gaze to roam over her features. A slight tinge of pink graced her pale cheeks, which perfectly complemented the colour of her bow-shaped lips. How had she bewitched him so easily? He first set eyes upon her at the assembly, and by the end of the party at Lucas Lodge, he had been ensnared by her wit and her charm.

"You are too quiet," she said as she opened one eye. "Have I shocked you?"

"No, I am not put off by your confession." Should he tell her what had truly preoccupied him?

Her other eye opened, and she watched him for a moment. "Do you object to courting such a graceless creature?"

His head tilted slightly. "Graceless? I would never describe you as such."

"I am unsure if I should ask how you would, then."

"When you closed your eyes, I found enjoyment in watching your happiness in the moment. You have an elegance I find pleasing." He stepped forward and took her gloved hand, cradling it in his own. "No other lady has captured me as you have."

"Mr. Darcy," she said almost too soft to hear.

"I know we are not betrothed, but when it is just the two of us, could you not address me as Fitzwilliam?"

She glanced behind him, likely at the maid who followed. "Sir?"

"And no 'sir.' I am not some stranger or elder you must be subservient to. I desire to know what you think—what you feel." Her hand possessed a quiver he had failed to notice before now. He set her hand upon his arm and continued along the path that circled the pond. "Forgive me if I make you uneasy."

"You puzzle me exceedingly. I confess I had little success in sketching your character in Hertfordshire. I believe I have seen more of your true nature with Georgiana and your cousin." She stopped and turned and took in a deep inhale. "May I ask a question of you?"

"You have asked me several since we met in London. I hope you know I have naught to hide from you." She had a difficult time holding his eye. What could she need to ask that would make her so ill-at-ease?

"When I made the acquaintance of Mr. Wickham, he mentioned that he had grown up at your estate, Pemberley."

"Yes, his father was my father's steward and an excellent man." His free hand clenched at his side and his teeth ground against each other. He could well imagine what Wickham told her.

"He claimed you cheated him of a living provided by your father. I have come to believe he is not what he seems since he claimed Georgiana to be proud. Your sister is kind and gentle. I cannot understand why he would wish to malign her in such a way." She shook her head and swallowed hard. "Forgive me, but I do not know how to ask..."

"Do not distress yourself." His hand covered hers on his arm as he told her the history between George Wickham and himself. Miss Elizabeth was not a timid creature, but Wickham's action could cause anyone disquiet. When he concluded the tale, she blinked back tears that pooled along her bottom lashes.

"How could I have been so blind?" She pressed her palm to her chest. "How could he attempt to harm you and Georgiana? I am afraid I must beg your forgiveness. After the assembly, I listened to his claims and never questioned why he would share such personal information with me."

He took her hand and pressed a kiss to her knuckles. "Pray, must we discuss Wickham? After the manner in which I treated you, I cannot fault you for giving credit to his lies, but I would much prefer you come to know me instead of discussing what is in the past." He tugged her to continue along the pathway. "I also desire to know of your father."

"My father?"

"I hope to one day ask his permission to marry you. I plan to travel to Hertfordshire to speak to him soon and do not wish to catch him unawares." She faced straight ahead, so the curls of her fringe and the side of her bonnet were all that was visible at the moment. "Would there be anything that could help me win his permission?"

A laugh burst from her, and she tilted her head to look at him. "Do you wish to buy his acceptance?"

"No, but perhaps smooth the way a bit." He smiled at the melodic sound of her amusement.

"Perhaps if you speak to him of your feelings for me, similar to how you do so to me, you will convince him. For what it is worth, he trusts my uncle implicitly."

He winced. When he confessed his feelings to her, he shook as a leaf might before falling from its limb. How could he be so free with her father? "Perhaps a bottle of French brandy and that volume of Shelley. I could see if Hatchard's or Temple of Muses has a copy. You said he had been unable to procure that volume."

Her laugh filled the air and made his heart swell in his chest as it had never done before. "Brandy and a book would work well too, but take great care. He may want to court you if you are not careful, though I daresay he could be an agreeable partner."

He shook his head. How he wanted to stop her mouth with a kiss!

Chapter 9

The door to the palatial house opened before she could knock, and a thin man with a white tuft of a moustache ushered her inside from the cold. "Good morning, Miss Bennet," he said as he took her pelisse and gloves. While she handed him her bonnet, she could not help how her eyes darted about the hall, taking in the ceiling, the elegant vase on the table, and the painting on the far wall. How would she ever become accustomed to such finery? To be Mrs. Darcy would certainly be more than she had ever dreamt! "Miss Darcy is in the music room—"

"Miss Elizabeth!" She spun around to Fitzwilliam, who stood in an open doorway, an endearing smile upon his countenance. "We were to depart in a half hour to Cheapside. You have anticipated us."

"Did you not receive my uncle's message?" She had to be thankful they were so early. Otherwise, the Darcys may have been travelling to Cheapside when she arrived at their home.

"I did not," he said, stepping closer and turning to the butler. "Thank you, Watson. I shall show Miss Elizabeth to the music room." The man peered back and forth between them before hurrying off. As soon as he disappeared into the servants' passages, Fitzwilliam turned back to her.

She breathed in an even manner in an effort to calm the fluttering he caused. "My uncle had business in Mayfair, so he delivered me here before continuing on. He saw no reason for you and Georgiana to spend all that unnecessary time in a carriage. He does ask that you return me to his home this evening."

"Well, I have no complaints when we have you with us for longer than we would have otherwise." He took her hand and bestowed a soft kiss to the back. Between the theatre and the two walks they had taken since they met again in London, she was accustomed to him touching her hand with gloves. The lack was a shock as was the jolt that coursed through her at the intimate contact.

After a shaky breath, she forced her attention back to his face. "How was your journey to Hertfordshire?"

His free hand covered their joined ones. "The weather was as pleasant as I could expect for December. Despite your uncle's letter warning your father of my arrival, I seem to have caused a great deal of uproar."

"My father likely withheld the information from my mother. He will do so for his own amusement at her surprise, then becomes irritated with the disturbance. I apologise if Mama was... exuberant." How mortifying! When excited, her mother's rantings and ravings could be heard from outside the house, even when closed up tightly for the winter weather. He could not have escaped her loud proclamations.

"I was not much in her company. I was brought to your father's book room where we spoke. He penned you a letter. I have it on my desk." He tugged her into the next room while she cast her eyes about in an attempt to view as much as she could.

"Elizabeth," he said. He smiled and held out the letter when she turned. "If you like, Georgiana and I could give you a tour of the house."

"Forgive me." She withdrew her hand from his to take the letter and put it in her reticule. "Your home is lovely."

He stepped closer. "I hope you are comfortable."

She nodded in haste. "Yes, I am. I am merely not accustomed to... 'Tis a little overwhelming."

"Have you started the Shelley?"

"I have, but I have yet to read enough to discuss the work well." His proximity made her heart stutter in her chest. Did he just step a bit closer? She glanced around, her eyes settling on a portrait over the mantel. "Are those your parents?"

"They are." Fitzwilliam appeared much like his father, tall with dark chestnut hair, but his eyes were identical to his mother's.

"They were a handsome couple. Georgiana bears a great resemblance to your mother." She hazarded a glance back at him, but he was looking at the painting.

"She does. Her voice in the past few years has become similar as well." When his gaze returned to her, he lifted her hand to his lips once more. "You are trembling." His fingers took to grazing across her palm in a way that created gooseflesh all over.

"I do that when I am with you. I do not understand it. I have never felt so before." She cleared her throat and attempted to divert her mind from what he was doing to her hand. "But in Hertfordshire, I do not believe I was indifferent. I have never become so intemperate over an idle comment. You angered me in a way I have never experienced. I did not know what to do."

"You drew my eye at every event," he said softly. "I searched for your laugh in the voices around me, your curls bobbing around the dance floor, and the grace of your figure as you moved about the room with Miss Bingley." His thumb grazed along her jawline. "You need not do a thing to earn my regard. You have had it for some time. I only ask for the opportunity to earn your good opinion—to earn your love."

"Brother?" Elizabeth jumped back from Fitzwilliam as though scalded while Georgiana looked back and forth between them. "Oh, forgive me." She began to walk away, but Elizabeth hastened after her.

"Georgiana, you need not leave. We were talking, nothing more. Your brother did not receive my uncle's message last night and wished to give me a letter from my father."

The girl turned around and crossed her arms over her chest. "You are certain?"

"Yes, Poppet," said Fitzwilliam. "I would have brought Miss Elizabeth to you in a minute or two, but since you are here, I shall leave the two of you to your decorating. I have correspondence to attend to." His eyes met Elizabeth's one more time before Georgiana took her arm and pulled her into one of the drawing rooms.

"I am so happy you have joined me," said Georgiana, clasping her hands in front of her. "Brother said we are not to climb ladders, so I thought we would put the holly on the mantelpieces and what we can accomplish without climbing. I shall call for a footman once we have the kissing bough prepared."

Elizabeth bit her cheek to keep from laughing. He had not informed her of that small dictate but left it to his sister to mention. As much as she despised being told what to do, she had little desire to break an arm or a leg and be confined for Christmastide, so she would not argue—this time.

"I beg your pardon for interrupting, Miss Darcy." They both looked up from the table of holly in front of them to the housekeeper in the doorway. "Miss Bingley has called, Miss."

"Can I not send her away?" Georgiana's face contorted into a grimace.

Elizabeth spluttered out a laugh. "Do you not care for the lady?"

"I never would have said so before, but no. You must understand that she calls on me and rattles away for the entirety of the visit or asks questions about Fitzwilliam. I do not think she even pauses to take a breath. Her scheme to wed Fitzwilliam is obvious, so she seeks to endear herself to me as well as use me to become closer to him." She reached around to untie the apron she wore to protect her gown.

"Here, let me help you."

After they both removed their aprons, Georgiana grabbed Elizabeth's wrist. "You must come with me. After all, you are acquainted with Miss Bingley. Perhaps she will depart with haste once she understands her suit is all but lost."

"I do not know if that alone will frighten her away," said Elizabeth. She wanted to greet Miss Bingley as much as Georgiana did.

As they entered the drawing room, Miss Bingley stood with an affected smile upon her countenance. "Miss Darcy! I realised last night that I have not called upon you in ages. I had no intention of slighting you, my dear. I do hope you can forgive me." Her eyes shifted to Elizabeth and the false cheer dropped from her expression like a lead weight. "Eliza Bennet? I was unaware you were in London."

Elizabeth rose from her curtsey and narrowed her eyes. "I am curious as to how that is possible. If you remember, you accepted my sister Jane's call then visited my aunt and uncle's home on Gracechurch Street to return their call. I passed you in the hall when I brought the children back from their walk." A tiny squeak came from Georgiana, but Elizabeth managed to keep her expression from altering.

The lady pursed her lips with a sniff. "Forgive me. It must have slipped my mind."

"Of course," said Elizabeth. "I hope your brother and sister are well." She glanced at Georgiana as they stepped over to the sofa and sat down. "I was pleased your brother could join us for supper on Saturday evening. The production of Hamlet was well done, do you not agree?"

Miss Bingley gave a tiny cough, then pressed a hand to her chest. "I confess I did not watch much of the play. I could not care less about what occurs on the stage. I go to the theatre to see and be seen as does anyone of *quality*."

"Such a shame to have missed such a splendid performance." Elizabeth turned to Georgiana. "I believe Mr. Darcy said this production was the best he had seen thus far." She pressed her lips together as she turned back to the scarlet complexion of Miss Bingley. "He was quite impressed as I recall."

Georgiana nodded with a slight curve to her lips. "He was indeed. He also greatly enjoyed the company of you and your family. He has spoken of it more than once since."

"He was gracious to include us, as you were when you invited me to spend the day with you today."

Miss Bingley's eyebrows rose, and her eyes widened in a gradual fashion as Elizabeth spoke. "Spend the day?" she muttered softly.

"Nonsense!" said Georgiana, following Elizabeth's lead. "Since you and my brother are courting, I wish to know you better. After all, I have never seen my brother as determined as he has been of late, so I am certain we shall be sisters. You should also become accustomed to Darcy House. We want you to be comfortable here when you the two of you are wed. After all, this will be your home too."

"Courting!" Miss Bingley shot out of her chair, her fists clenched tightly at her sides. "You must be joking."

Georgiana lifted her eyebrows. "I would never jest over such a thing. Elizabeth is my friend, and my brother is courting her. Why would that be a laughing matter?"

"Why, do you not know how she will be excluded from the drawing rooms of the *ton*? Her family is every bit ridiculous. Do you not know of her connections?"

"What I know, Miss Bingley, is that my friend is a gentleman's daughter and my brother is a gentleman." Georgiana held Miss Bingley's gaze while she stood. "Her uncle and aunt have better manners and are more pleasing than many of those in the *ton*." Elizabeth grabbed at Georgiana's hand but missed. While she appreciated the girl's defence, she could not allow her to continue. What if Georgiana went too far? "My brother and I would prefer their company to many we tolerate due to rank or who their brother is." Elizabeth finally snagged Georgiana's hand just as the girl's opposite hand landed on her hip. She was too late.

Miss Bingley clutched her reticule with both hands as a simpering smile overtook her features. "Now, Miss Darcy, you are young and do not understand—"

"Miss Bingley," said Georgiana, her hand quaking. "I understand that you have called upon me for years in an attempt to ingratiate yourself not only to me, but also my brother. He has never held any sort of interest in you and will never offer you marriage." She inhaled and drew herself a bit taller. "I have always accepted your calls out of respect for your brother, but I shall not tolerate such disrespect for my brother, myself, or my friend in my own home. Pray, do not call again. You will not be admitted."

"What?" Miss Bingley blanched, and her knuckles whitened from the increase of her grip upon the ribbons of her poor reticule. "You would never. Your brother will not allow it!"

"I will not allow what, may I ask?"

Elizabeth's heart dropped into her stomach at the sight of Fitzwilliam in the doorway. What would he think of Georgiana's outburst, not to mention her edict? Would he blame her for his younger sister's uncharacteristic behaviour?

Miss Bingley marched a few steps closer to him. "I called upon your sister to enjoy a talk between friends, only to discover Eliza Bennet is here. Imagine my surprise when your sister claimed you to be courting that lady. I, of course, expressed my doubt over the matter when your sister insulted me and said I would no longer be admitted to your home."

He looked over to them. "Is this true?"

Elizabeth opened her mouth, but before she could speak, Georgiana stomped past her. "Brother, she insulted Elizabeth and insinuated I am naïve. I merely informed her that I knew of her motive for calling upon me and told her I would no longer be accepting her visits." By the end, Georgiana stood by her brother's side with her arms crossed upon her chest.

Fitzwilliam rocked back onto his heels and clasped his hands behind his back. "Miss Bingley, I can only imagine what you could have said to receive such a scene from my sister. Your brother has mentioned on more than one occasion of your hopes in regard to marriage, and I responded with the same answer on each and every occasion—that you would never receive an offer from me. I have never desired a confrontation over the matter or to be rude to the relation of a good friend, yet if you are to enter my home and insult the lady I am courting, as well as Georgiana for her desire to become better acquainted with her, then I must agree with my sister. I must ask that you depart."

"But—"

"Miss Bingley, I hope this house to one day be Miss Elizabeth's as well. I shall not allow anyone to insult her in her own home." The lady's face contorted into a sneer as she glanced back at Elizabeth and strode from the room without another word.

After the front door slammed shut, Fitzwilliam rubbed his hands up his face then through his hair. "I wonder if that will be the end of it." He sighed, shook his head, then laughed. "I must say, Georgiana, I am surprised, to say the least."

"I am sorry, Brother, but from the moment she set eyes on Elizabeth, she was determined to be awful. I do not believe I have ever been so angry with someone."

Elizabeth pressed her hand to her forehead. He laughed, but what if he was actually angry? "I must beg your forgiveness as well. Her first words when she saw me were that she did not know I was in London, and I called her out on her falsehood. I fear Georgiana followed my lead."

"Do not have a care," he said with a smile. He hugged his sister, then with his arm still around her shoulders, took Elizabeth's hand, pulling her from the sofa. "I do not blame you." He leaned a little to the side to ensure he caught Elizabeth's eye. "You put up with Miss Bingley's rather pointed barbs and veiled insults at Netherfield and did so with humour. I am certain you did not set out to lambaste her."

Georgiana's face wrinkled and she pursed her lips. "Do you like to be addressed as Eliza?"

"My friend Charlotte Lucas and her family began calling me Eliza when I came out. The name never bothered me at the time, but Miss Bingley says it as though it is something filthy. I also never gave her permission to address me so informally. If I am to be honest, her tone alone makes me grit my teeth." She gave a bit of a shrug. "You should probably know my uncle penned a letter last night to Mr. Bingley."

"I know your sister was undecided in regard to him after the theatre and supper," said Fitzwilliam. "Has she made a decision?"

"My aunt and I discussed the matter at length with her yesterday. I believe if not for our courtship, she would have refused his request to call long before now. I had to assure her the decision she made would have no bearing on our understanding." Pulling Jane's teeth would have been less difficult than prying out the truth of her feelings. What a chore that had been! "After the theatre, Mr. Bingley seemed astounded during supper to learn we have been in London, and he implied his sisters merely forgot to mention her presence to him. Considering how hurt she was by those ladies, Jane did not press him, but her faith in him is shaken. He lost a great deal of her respect by his wilful blindness. I believe my aunt made her see that she needed to speak of her decision after inquiring if she could spend the rest of her life in the same home as Miss Bingley."

Georgiana shuddered. "I am thankful Miss Bingley never managed to force Fitzwilliam's hand. That would have been horrible."

"And you would not have been the one wed to the lady," said Fitzwilliam. "Not that I would have ever agreed to any scheme to save her reputation. I would have preferred to be known as an unrepentant rake."

His sister rolled her eyes. "Well, for one, I am relieved that was never necessary."

Elizabeth arched her one eyebrow. "I am as well. If you were known as a rake, my uncle may not have welcomed your suit with such ease."

"I do not believe the predicament would have been an obstacle."

"No?"

He laughed and shook his head. "No, since I would have just introduced him to Miss Bingley. He would have understood and granted me permission without delay."

A bark of amusement burst from her. "You are quite ridiculous."

"No," he said simply. "I am happy."

Chapter 10

As much as Darcy had wished to keep Elizabeth in his home until he could obtain her acceptance of his hand, if not longer, he and Georgiana returned her to Gracechurch Street in time for supper, and at Mrs. Gardiner's invitation, remained to sup with them.

He sat quietly during their return to Darcy House, the dark of the carriage allowing him to close his eyes and imagine Elizabeth's warm smile and laugh to soothe the ache of leaving her behind in Cheapside. What he would not give to have her at his side, already his wife! He had questioned every word from his mouth in her presence until he surrendered to what was in his heart and let his feelings fall freely from his lips. In some manner, he was more relaxed since he let go of his reservations, since he let himself love her.

Watson stood stiff, worrying his hands, when they stepped into the hall. "Mr. Bingley arrived during your absence, sir. I tried to persuade him to come again on the morrow, but he was not having it. He insisted upon awaiting your return."

"Do not let him unsettle you. After my sister set down his today, I expected him to call sooner rather than later."

"Brother?" said Georgiana, her eyes wide.

"I shall speak to him, Poppet. He must understand his sister cannot continue to assume I shall one day make her my wife. I was content to ignore her using her brother's friendship with me to ingratiate herself with you as well as garner invitations to events, but now that I am courting Miss Elizabeth, I cannot permit her insinuations to continue. This conversation needed to happen, regardless of what occurred today."

Georgiana watched the floor while she nodded. She had apologised on several occasions since the confrontation with Miss Bingley, as had Elizabeth, yet as he had told them both, their remorse was unnecessary. This day would have come with or without his sister standing up to the lady. If anything, he was proud of her for defending Elizabeth, as well as speaking her mind. How many people could take advantage of Georgiana if she refused to stand up to them? No, his baby sister needed to grow up. The events of today meant someone like Wickham would be less likely to touch her naïve sensibilities in the future. How could he not celebrate that maturity?

Once she disappeared into the music room, he stepped into the drawing room where Bingley stood before the fire with his arms crossed over his chest. "You can be at no loss as to why I have come."

Darcy shook his head. "No, I knew you would come, though I admit to hoping you would wait until after Christmastide to do so. We have spoken of your sister and her aspirations, Bingley. I have never wavered on my convictions or on her unsuitability as my wife. I do not care for her, and I do not appreciate her finding humour at the expense of others. She is cruel and manipulative, and I would never commit to spending a lifetime with her. You were supposed to convince her of my adamant belief that we would never suit."

His friend's shoulders dropped, and he rubbed his forehead. "I thought you would one day change your mind."

"What?" Had his jaw just hit the floor? "I have never altered in my opinion. I told you—"

"Yes, yes, but you also have never made any effort to engage a lady. You offend them at every turn and oft times seek to rebuff them. Caroline has been the sole lady you have never sought to alienate."

"Because she is your sister," said Darcy with a raised voice. "I endured her pretentions and fawning attentions while begging you to speak to her because she *is* your sister. Our friendship has been the reason she has continued to be admitted to my homes and maintained the ability to use my name to procure invitations to the parlours and drawing rooms of the *ton*. I have never been ignorant of her actions, even though my aunt Lady Fitzwilliam has insisted on more than one occasion for me to put an end to the connection. I never did so out of respect for you."

Bingley covered his face and inhaled deeply, the air hissing through his fingers. He let his hands slide down his face before they dropped to his sides. "This is irrelevant. The *ton* has linked the two of you for some time. If you do not wed my sister, she will be a laughingstock—she will be ruined—"

"I have told you for years that I would never wed your sister, and I never dissembled. I have also never heard one rumour of a match between me and your sister. Even if I were linked to her, the gossip columns have paired me with more than one young lady over a mere set at a ball. Should I have wed each of them?" Darcy shook his head. "I am not exaggerating when I say that should your sister ever be discovered in this home without a stitch of clothing upon her body, I would leave her to her ruin. I have done all in my power to convince you of this, but as you have said this evening, you did naught to prevent this eventuality. Any consequences to Miss Bingley's reputation are on your head." Bingley could not be surprised, could he? He had been warned.

"But—"

"Your sister insulted the lady I am courting in my home and in front of my sister. If anything, I am exceedingly proud of Georgiana for defending Miss Elizabeth and doing what should have been done a long time ago."

Bingley scoffed. "You cannot be serious! You are to truly court Miss Elizabeth Bennet? I noticed your marked attention at the supper after the theatre, but you must know how the lady despises you." He gave an odd twitch and narrowed his eyes. "Besides, you said yourself that the family is unsuitable. You claimed she was 'tolerable, but not handsome enough to tempt you.'"

They both startled at the door opening, and Richard entering with a crooked grin. "Do my ears deceive me or do I hear a puppy crying?" His cousin had never tolerated Bingley, and Bingley enjoyed being called a "puppy" even less.

"Bloody hell, you are an arse, Fitzwilliam," said Bingley in a growl.

"I happened upon my young cousin in the hall, and she informed me of what transpired earlier today. You cannot be surprised, Bingley. Darcy has told you forever he would never wed her. I have been present on several of those occasions."

Darcy sighed and leaned against a nearby chair. "He is attempting to claim I am honour bound to marry her."

"Like hell you are." Richard flashed a terrible frown at Bingley and pointed directly at the younger man's chest. "You should watch your step. My mother and father have been quite unhappy with your sister's behaviour in regard to my cousin for years. You had best rein her in now before you are ruined by association."

"Whatever do you mean?" Bingley's tone held a haughtiness Darcy had never heard before.

"I mean my parents will not hesitate to protect their own, and if she receives the cut direct from those of a higher circle, you will be ruined along with her." Richard did not embellish or speak with passion. The statement was made as one would relay a fact.

"You do realise he courts Miss Elizabeth when he warned me against the elder sister? If Miss Bennet is so unworthy, what makes her sister so different?"

Darcy raised himself to his full height. Since when did Bingley know how to sneer? "You should listen to yourself. When you begged for my opinion of Miss Bennet, I told you I never saw any hint of particular regard, which was true. I did not know until I happened upon Miss Elizabeth in London that her sister's feelings ran deeper than that of acquaintances." Bingley made to speak, but Darcy shifted closer. "*You* decided to return to London, and your sisters followed by design. If you recall, I told you Miss Bingley penned a letter to Miss Bennet implying you would soon be betrothed to Georgiana."

His cousin hissed through his teeth. "I do not know what she is about, but if she taints Georgiana in any way, the Fitzwilliams will know how to act."

Bingley's eyes widened. "I have never thought of—that is to say, I would never—"

"Your sisters received Miss Bennet's call a week after your return from Hertfordshire," said Darcy without acknowledging Bingley's denial towards the statements regarding Georgiana. "They even returned the call. They journeyed to Gracechurch Street two weeks later where they were abominably rude to not only Miss Bennet, but also Mrs. Gardiner." When he took one more step towards Bingley, the smaller man stepped back, nearly stumbling over a table. "You approached me at the theatre wanting to be reintroduced to Miss Bennet. I invited you to supper, giving you the chance to redeem yourself. I understand Miss Bennet has decided against you, but you have no one to blame for that but yourself."

"Has she?" Richard's eyebrows were raised. "I cannot say I blame her."

"Miss Elizabeth told you?" said Bingley in a weak tone.

"She did. She also told me her sister's decision was in part due to your sister. Her aunt asked if she would desire to spend her life in the same home as Miss Bingley."

Richard guffawed and clapped his hands together. "Forgive me, but I cannot be surprised at her decision when presented with such a dilemma." Darcy had to agree with his cousin. He had experienced the exact same sentiment when he first met Bingley's sister. Hurst's near-constant inebriated state was surely due to the misery of living with not just Mrs. Hurst but having Miss Bingley in their company all day every day.

"You must marry her, Darcy." Bingley's hands were clenched at his sides, and he stood rigid, but his voice was unconvincing.

"What will you do, Bingley?" Richard crossed his arms over his chest and kicked out a foot. "Will you call my cousin out? He is a better shot than you, and he has bested you how often with a blade? You would be a blunderbuss to challenge him. He would put you down within minutes."

Bingley began to bounce, his jaw working while his eyes darted back and forth between Richard and Darcy until eventually, he broke and hurried towards the door. Richard wiggled his fingers in a ridiculous wave. "Have a lovely evening," he called. Once the door slammed, Richard laughed. "'Tis past time you excised that boil from your arse."

"I cannot credit that he assumed I would one day surrender and wed his sister." The notion confounded him. The thought of Miss Bingley as his wife prompted a shudder to roll down his spine. "Bingley has always been weak, particularly with his sisters, but I never recognised he was a coward in every sense of the word."

Richard poured a sizeable glass of brandy and took a large swallow. "I cannot claim to be surprised. He has never put Miss Bingley in her place, else she would not behave so. She will humiliate him one day, and he will be finished before he has even purchased an estate."

"She believes the Bennets to be so beneath them, yet even with an estate, Bingley will not be the Bennets' equal. That family has possessed Longbourn for centuries and have mere links to trade. Bingley still maintains ownership of his factories in the north and if he ever acquires an estate, he will be newly landed.

"Miss Bennet would have been an excellent match for him." His cousin dropped into a chair near the fire and crossed an ankle over his knee. "I maintain she is too good for him. He is a weasel who latched onto you to elevate himself socially.

Mother and Father will be thrilled to hear of today's events in regard to him as well as his sister. Miss Bingley once sniffed about Carlisle, and my mother was adamant Miss Bingley would never succeed her as Lady Fitzwilliam."

"I do not believe this will be the last we hear from Bingley." He hated to harm Bingley, but if he and his sister behaved as usual, the possibility was not implausible. The Bingley he knew would behave as if naught occurred, yet tonight, he witnessed shades of the man he never knew existed. That Bingley may still harbour the same assumptions, or he may harbour resentment. He mentioned Miss Bennet more than once. He could regret his mistakes and seek someone to blame other than himself or his sisters. Regardless, Bingley would not attack Darcy to his face. "His sister will be more tenacious."

"She will," said Richard. "May I speak to my mother of this? She would be pleased to coordinate what needs to occur to minimise any ill-effects to Miss Elizabeth's reputation. The *ton* will have reservations with Miss Elizabeth's lack of fortune, though I believe the connection to Mr. Gardiner will not harm her as much as another relation who may come from trade. He has a profitable business and the respect of many in the peerage."

"Speak to your mother. I shall not allow Miss Bingley nor her brother to slander Elizabeth. She will be my wife, and I will protect her whether we have exchanged vows or not. She will not come to harm if I can prevent it."

Chapter 11

The morning dawned frigid in comparison to the days leading up to Christmas, the chill evident in the frost clinging to the window as well as the biting cold that penetrated the glass when Elizabeth stood too close. With a light touch, she pressed her fingertips to the window, melting the ice and leaving a clear mark when she pulled them away.

"Lizzy, come sit by the fire," said Jane, who had paused from reading *Goody Two Shoes* to Jemima.

Even though Elizabeth's gown covered her arms to her wrist, she grabbed her shawl and wrapped it around her. Between her sleeves and the wrap, she would not become ill—she refused. She had too much to anticipate in the weeks to come. Besides, she could not leave the window. She wanted to know the moment Fitzwilliam arrived.

"Watching will not make him come any sooner," said Aunt Gardiner with a hint of a smile. "I daresay he stuffed his poor sister into a carriage the moment she completed her toilette."

"Aunt!" Jane laughed while Elizabeth rolled her eyes. "You are being silly. You know they were to attend church just as we did."

Elizabeth tapped her foot and crossed her arms over her chest. "What if he is angry over what occurred with Miss Bingley?"

Aunt Gardiner rested her needlework in her lap. "When he returned you home last night, he was not a man upset. He still observed you as he has since we first made his acquaintance. You also told us he chastised the lady after his sister did so. I do not believe he would think nothing of it at the time, then completely change his opinion."

"I cannot imagine him so alterable," said her uncle. "Can you?"

"No, I cannot."

The steady striking of horses' hooves against the road caused her to jerk her head back so she could see the street. He was here! She rushed to the hall and stood before the door, pinching her cheeks then straightening her skirt. Good grief! When had she become Lydia? Well, maybe she was not so much like her youngest sister. Lydia would surely adjust her bosom and not her skirt.

After a deep breath, she opened the door as Fitzwilliam's foot hit the pavement. "Happy Christmas!" Her breath created a white cloud that floated away on the breeze. "I hope your journey was not too cold."

He handed out Georgiana with a slight lift to his lips. "We wore our warmest coats and the grooms heated bricks for us. We were quite comfortable, I assure you."

As they stepped towards the door, a footman followed with a small trunk. "What is this?" asked Elizabeth.

Fitzwilliam glanced at his sister with his smile widening. "You will see soon enough." Once they entered and had removed their coats and hats, Georgiana hurried into the drawing room while she and Fitzwilliam lingered behind. "You were waiting at the window?"

"I was." Why were her cheeks so warm? "I admit to fretting about what occurred with Miss Bingley yesterday. I fear I have driven my aunt and Jane to distraction."

His strong hand took hers with a gentleness she had once not considered him capable of possessing and bestowed a kiss to her knuckles. "Bingley awaited me when I returned last night."

A pang ripped through her chest. What if she caused their friendship to end? Would he blame her? "I hope he understood."

Fitzwilliam lifted his eyebrows while he retained his hold of her hand. "No, I am afraid he did not, but I would much prefer to delay this conversation for now. I promise I am not upset with you or Georgiana, but today is a happy occasion. Perhaps we can speak of it later."

She nodded and tried her best to cease that persistent niggle pestering her that something was amiss. They would speak of it, and he was not angry. That was what mattered most.

When they entered the drawing room, her aunt stood and clasped her hands in front of her. "Happy Christmas!" Her children, husband, and Jane all echoed her greeting before they bowed and curtseyed. Elizabeth grinned at Georgiana, who must have been immediately snatched by Jemima since the little girl sat on Georgiana's lap and held the book in front of her. Beatrice curtseyed with her parents, the needlework her mother was teaching her abandoned on the sofa.

"Would you care for some wassail?" Aunt looked between their guests. "I can also offer tea, coffee, or chocolate if you prefer." After Georgiana requested chocolate and Fitzwilliam coffee, they joined the others seated near the fire. At a gesture from Fitzwilliam, the footman set the small trunk beside him, bowed, and hurried from the room.

"Mrs. Gardiner, I hope I do not overstep, but I brought gifts for everyone."

"You should not have gone to such trouble," said Aunt Gardiner. The children each perked up and watched their mother.

"'Twas no bother; I assure you. I am grateful for the invitation to spend the day with your family." He flipped the lid and pulled out two small packages he handed to Georgiana. "My sister selected the gifts for the children." He withdrew the next two, which he handed to Mrs. Gardiner and Jane, followed by the last that he handed to her uncle.

When he held Elizabeth's before her, she winced and bit her lip. "But I have nothing for you."

"Never fear, my dear," said her uncle. "I can help you select something from my stock."

Fitzwilliam set the parcel in her lap. "I did not select this gift in expectation of one in return. Pray, do not feel obligated. Being here today is a gift to me."

She glanced to the children. Beatrice had forgotten her sewing in favour of the ball and cup she must have removed from the paper, now discarded beside her needlework. Jemima unfolded the wrapping with great care and gasped. "A doll! She is so pretty. Mama, look at her gown."

Her aunt smiled and fingered the silk folds. "I wonder if Miss Darcy made your doll and her gown. Pray, make sure you thank her. If she made her, she spent a prodigious amount of time on her."

"Thank you," said Beatrice, taking her eyes from her new toy for but a moment. Elizabeth pressed her lips together to keep from laughing. While Jemima more resembled Jane in demeanour, Beatrice oft times reminded Elizabeth of herself at that age.

Jemima's wide eyes looked up at Georgiana. "Thank you. Did you make her?"

"I did. One of my governesses taught me how to make dolls out of fabric scraps and sometimes even my old gowns. This was a gown I became too tall for and had only worn a handful of times. The doll's body and face are the underdress and her gown is a recreation of the one I used to make her."

Her small cousin touched the ribbon around the waist. "Will you teach me to make one someday?" Elizabeth pressed her hand to her chest at Jemima's sweet countenance and heartfelt request. She was such a good child. If she remained unaltered, she would be just like Jane when she grew up.

"Of course," said Georgiana. "I would enjoy teaching you."

Aunt Gardiner and Jane both exclaimed over their beautiful white embroidered shawls as Uncle thanked Fitzwilliam for the rare edition of Shakespeare. While Elizabeth fingered the tie on her own gift, the cheerful voices of her family surrounded her. She adored that sound. Their laughter and joyful countenances were the best part of the season, not to mention that the Gardiners' home was a great deal happier than Longbourn lately. She did not miss her mother's laments over Mr. Bingley's departure or her own refusal of Mr. Collins. She could be nothing but thankful her father agreed to their removal to town.

"Will you not open yours?" She lifted her eyes to those of Fitzwilliam's, who watched her with a soft expression.

"Lizzy," said her aunt, "if you would prefer, you and Mr. Darcy may go to your uncle's study." She dipped her chin down a bit. "The door should remain open."

After Fitzwilliam stood, he offered her his hand. "Thank you, Mrs. Gardiner." She stood but held her gift with both of her hands rather than placing one upon his arm. When they were alone, she set the wrapped package on the desk. "Does something displease you?"

"No, I simply feel remiss in not having something for you."

"I wish you would not. I am truly not concerned." He pressed the gift closer to her. "Pray, open it."

With shaky fingers, she tugged the string and let it fall open before she drew the paper away. A gasp escaped her. "'Tis stunning." She took a corner of the India shawl and lifted, but he stayed her hand.

"Careful. I wrapped something inside of it."

At his warning, she peeled back the layers of fabric to reveal a small box. She glanced at him before she picked it up and lifted the lid. "What a lovely comb." She drew the delicate silver piece from the material protecting it. "Would you put it in my hair?"

He cradled the ornament in his palm while she turned. "I am unsure of how to do this."

"I trust you. Place it where you think it will look best."

Once the teeth of the comb slid against her scalp, his finger brushed down the back of her neck. "I was correct. The silver complements the ebony of your hair."

She struggled to ignore that gooseflesh he created while she turned and wrapped the shawl around her shoulders. "How do I look?"

"Lovely," he said. He snagged a corner of the wrap and rubbed it between his fingers. "My mother loved India shawls. My father gave her this one for her birthday. She did not wear it much before she became too ill."

Her heart cracked and bled for him and Georgiana. The pain they must have endured losing both of their parents within a few years of each other. "Are you certain you wish me to have such a cherished keepsake? Georgiana may desire to wear it one day."

"No, she has her favourites, and when I asked of her feelings, she mentioned this one specifically." He cleared his throat and blinked. "We should return. I do not want to test your uncle's patience."

He made to turn, but she grasped him by the sleeve. "Fitzwilliam?" Before she could give it much thought, she rose to her tiptoes and kissed his cheek, her heart beating in a mad cadence against her ribs. What if she fainted? How horrifying would that be!

She hastened ahead of him without looking at him, but when she reached the hall, a hand to her elbow kept her from walking any further. She turned to his wide grin and a finger pointing towards the ceiling. When she lifted her head, a kissing bough hung just outside the study door, beckoning for a wayward couple to be caught underneath. "I had not noticed when we first passed. I believe 'tis bad luck to do so once much less twice. We should not tempt fate." Her eyes were surely as wide as saucers. Did he mean to kiss her—as in a real kiss?

His face crept closer and closer until she could not hold his gaze any longer and let her eyes flutter closed. Her heart was going to burst from her chest. His warm breath fanned against her cheek, only increasing the disconcerting light-headedness. When his lips caressed hers in the faintest of whispers, she inhaled a quick burst of air. A moment later, he was gone.

She opened her eyes and released her hand, which was squeezed impossibly tight around his mother's wrap. "Is that all?"

His low rumble filled the hall. "Is that all? Did you want there to be more?"

"You said we passed under the kissing bough once before. I thought we had to atone for our first passing as well."

His eyebrows shot up onto his forehead, and he stepped forward. "A good idea. We should certainly not leave anything to chance."

Her breath caught in her chest as his hand cupped her cheek, his thumb tracing along her cheekbone, while he bent forward. This time, her eyes closed a bit quicker, and his kiss was a bit firmer. She grasped his arms to keep from collapsing in a puddle at his feet but removed them with haste when he drew away.

At a tiny gasp, they both whipped around as a little head of tawny locks darted back inside the drawing room. "Mama! Papa! I saw Mr. Darcy kissing Cousin Lizzy under the kissing bough!"

Elizabeth pressed her palms to her burning cheeks while Fitzwilliam steepled his hands in front of his mouth, his shoulders shaking. This had to be the most horrifying moment of her life!

Chapter 12

The ledgers were spread across his desk, but he stared at them without seeing the numbers. He had made a grave error when kissing Elizabeth. For the entire two days since, he could not look at the kissing bough in his own hall without thinking of her—the way her vivid blue eyes fluttered closed, the way she ever-so-slightly leaned forward for his kiss, not to mention the sensation of his lips making contact with hers. Except for when he had cradled her cheek, he had fisted his hands at his sides to keep from wrapping his arms around her and pressing her as close to him as possible. The memory, while cherished, consumed him every moment of the day. Blast! He needed to rid himself of this preoccupation!

The door to the study swung open and Watson squeezed back against the panel as his aunt Lady Fitzwilliam strode inside as if the house was her own. "I am quite put out that you neglected to come to me when you made the important decision to court a lady."

"Lady—"

"Richard has spoken of your Miss Elizabeth in glowing terms, which we know he is not wont to do, so I must assume she has a brain in her head and a modicum of wit. But you need me. I should have escorted Miss Elizabeth around on calls as soon as you began courting her, but that is neither here nor there at this point. You must arrange for me to meet her, for we have a prodigious amount to accomplish before you announce a betrothal."

"Lady—"

"You will, of course, bring her to my Twelfth Night masquerade. Your uncle is acquainted with hers, so they may accompany her for the sake of propriety. He assures me Mr. and Mrs. Gardiner could be mistaken for people of fashion, so I am relying on his judgement in the matter."

He stood silent while they stared at one another. Was she done? Would he be interrupted again?

"Well?" she said in a higher pitch. "Do you not have anything to tell me?"

"Forgive me. I wanted to ensure you had said all you meant to say." He placed his pen beside the ledger. "I am grateful for any and all aid you are willing to bestow upon Miss Elizabeth. I had not planned on keeping our courtship quiet from you. I sought to improve her poor opinion of me and happened to do so quicker than I realised. I was so pleased, I neglected to tell anyone besides Richard and Georgiana."

"How does she get on with Georgiana?"

"They are good friends. Georgiana even set Miss Bingley down on Christmas Eve for insulting Miss Elizabeth."

Lady Fitzwilliam's serious expression changed as a crooked grin, resembling her son's, appeared upon her countenance. "Did she? I am pleased to hear it. Richard mentioned Miss Bingley was jealous of the match, but he had not told me of a set down. My sole concern with this development is Miss Bingley's penchant for gossip. From what Richard told me, her brother has assumed you will one day capitulate and offer her marriage. We are all well aware how she has insisted upon using your name since she entered society. If she does not desist, we must act."

He cringed. After what occurred three days ago, he wanted to forget the Bingleys existed, if only that were possible. "Could we not simply ensure she is excluded from any events you plan? That should inform her of our displeasure, particularly when I cease to associate with Bingley at my club."

The door opened once again without warning, to Richard, who strode inside and sat. "If you are speaking of White's, then you must know Bingley is there at this very moment, telling any and all who are willing to listen that you have abused his friendship and used his sister ill."

"He what?" Darcy dropped into his chair. "I have told him for years I would not marry his shrew of a sister, and I have never given her one ounce of encouragement. He is addled in the mind if he believes this will force my hand."

Richard shoved a glass of brandy into his grip. "Drink this before you collapse. I have never seen him so white," he said to Lady Fitzwilliam. "We need to avert his attempts to entrap you. I confronted Bingley as loudly as possible in front of everyone present to which he turned a fascinating shade of purple and spluttered in his defence. A few of father's allies came over and proclaimed they believed not a word of it, but others who thrive on this sort of discord were eager to spread the tale."

His mother scoffed. "I am sure they were." She rolled her eyes and tapped her fingernails against the desk. "We need to act quickly. When can you introduce me to Miss Elizabeth?"

"Today if you wish it. I am to depart for Cheapside in a half hour."

"Perfect," she said, examining her fingernails. "I plan to make a few calls on the morrow. If she can be persuaded to join me, then we shall begin."

"You are making calls during Christmastide?"

Richard snickered. "My mother would make calls on Sunday if she thought they would be accepted."

Lady Fitzwilliam reached over and pinched her son's arm. "I had a note from one friend who invited me to call, and I know of a few ladies who are accepting calls over Christmastide." She turned back to Darcy. "I understand you hosted this lady and her family at the theatre. You must be seen out with her again if possible. Perhaps she can be convinced to attend church with you and Georgiana on Sunday. We must send a clear message to all and sundry, repeating what Richard said at your club today. You have finally found a lady you feel worthy of being Mrs. Darcy, and Miss Bingley is insulted after her blatant pursuit of you for all of these years. Her and her brother's claims are naught but sour grapes." She grabbed Richard's arm. "I need you to fetch your father and inform him of what happened at White's. The three of you must act."

Darcy frowned. "What do you have planned?"

She gave a small titter. "If I know your uncle, he will have Mr. Bingley's membership revoked. Frankly, he may have leased an estate, but he holds no land. Your friendship was certain to have gained him admittance, but he has turned upon you. You need to disassociate yourself from him. He cannot continue to gain his legitimacy as a gentleman from you. He has traded in on your name for long enough." She pushed her son's arm. "Why are you standing about in such a stupid manner? Do you not have something to do?"

Richard sighed and held up his hand. "We shall speak this evening."

Before his cousin had closed the door, Lady Fitzwilliam frowned. "Did the two of you have something to discuss?"

With a shrug, Darcy closed his ledger and straightened his desk. "Not that I am aware of. He may have merely wished to tell me more of what Bingley said." He rang the bell. "I shall have the carriage brought around."

"Nonsense," said his aunt. "Why take the time to prepare your vehicle when mine sits at the kerb? Come, we may as well depart now. I am unsure why, but a number of people seem to be travelling about London today. You would not want to be late."

During the trip, Lady Fitzwilliam peppered Darcy with questions of Elizabeth's family, her accomplishments, as well as where he stood in his suit. What a trial! His aunt could never be compared to his mother's sister, Lady Catherine, yet she showed a similar officiousness today. Thankfully, Lady Fitzwilliam's interrogation was more well-meaning than Lady Catherine's would be. That was one relation who would be most displeased to learn of his courtship with Elizabeth, but even more so, of a betrothal.

"What a lovely home," said Lady Fitzwilliam when they stopped in front of the Gardiner's house. "Your uncle indicated Mr. Gardiner did well with his business, yet I never imagined."

"He mentioned to me once that he sells some of his wine and brandy to the Prince Regent."

"Indeed? Your uncle has not made mention of that."

When the servant opened the carriage door, he alighted, then helped her step to the pavement. The butler was quick to greet them and usher them inside. Meanwhile, his aunt cast her eye about the hall as though she had never set foot in a house before. Had she believed a wealthy tradesman's home would be different than her own?

Their coats were taken before they were announced. Poor Mrs. Gardiner paled at his aunt's entrance. "Fitzwilliam, do introduce us," said his aunt with ease.

"Lady Evelyn Fitzwilliam, may I present Mrs. Edward Gardiner, Miss Jane Bennet, and Miss Elizabeth Bennet." As he spoke, his aunt's eyes moved to each of the ladies with a welcome smile, which softened when she set eyes upon Miss Elizabeth.

"'Tis a pleasure to make your acquaintance." She looked to Mrs. Gardiner. "Pray forgive me for intruding upon my nephew's call, but I am afraid I appeared upon his doorstep and insisted I would join him."

"You charged into my study with the tact of a—"

"Yes, well, I should not have learnt you were courting a lady from my son." She stepped over to Elizabeth and took her hands. "I hope you do not find me presumptuous, but I am eager to know you better. Fitzwilliam mentioned your influence helped Georgiana rebuke Miss Bingley."

Elizabeth gasped. "No, my lady—"

"Do not deny it. If my niece felt inclined to protect you, then your influence played a part."

"Pray, do sit down," said Mrs. Gardiner, who seemed to have recovered her usual complexion. Darcy bristled when his aunt took the sole open seat by Elizabeth.

"As I was saying, with the censure of Miss Bingley, I believe we need to anticipate her gossip, so I was hoping you would be willing to accompany me on calls tomorrow."

Elizabeth's eyes bulged and she pressed a hand to her chest. "Calls? With you? I fear I would not know what to say—or what to do."

Lady Fitzwilliam patted the top of Elizabeth's hand. "Do not concern yourself, dear. You will simply follow my lead. I shall inform you of aught you need to know between stops." She glanced to Mrs. Gardiner. "Would you mind terribly if I stole away your niece for the day?"

"No, she may spend as much time with you as is required."

His beloved fidgeted with the fabric of her skirt, and was that a tiny tremble in her fingers? If only he could take Elizabeth back under that kissing bough and relieve her anxieties! Perhaps he should have sent a note ahead to warn her of his aunt's presence as well as her forthright nature.

"Excellent!" His aunt clasped her hands with a pleased expression. "Now, I must know more about you, but first, I want you to tell me how you met my nephew."

Elizabeth peeked over at him and pinked. "We met at an assembly while he was in Hertfordshire with Mr. Bingley."

"An assembly?" Lady Fitzwilliam giggled as though she was a girl of Jemima's age. "My nephew attended an assembly? I am certain he would rather have a tooth pulled, and to think, you are now courting. I can hardly credit it."

"May I enquire why that is so difficult to believe?"

"I have never met a more disagreeable person than Fitzwilliam when at a ball. His usual behaviour is to be as rude as possible to the ladies in attendance, so he need not dance with them."

Was this his turn for his face to catch fire? "Really, Aunt, 'tis not necessary."

When Elizabeth set eyes upon him, she began to laugh. "Forgive me," she said while shaking her head.

His aunt looked back and forth between them and rolled her eyes. "So, he was as impossible as ever."

"Yes, my lady," said Elizabeth before his aunt flashed him a knowing glance. He gave a silent groan. This would not do! He wanted this time with Elizabeth, not for her to be occupied with his aunt for the entirety of the call. How long would Lady Fitzwilliam persist in this useless questioning? He needed to find some method of ending this conversation before Elizabeth told her of the "tolerable" comment, lest his aunt plague him about that for the remainder of his days!

Chapter 13

With her hands clenched tightly in her lap, Elizabeth kept her eyes on the lady speaking, feigning an interest in the gossip dripping from her mouth like venom from one of those snakes she had read of that lived in India. Lady Fitzwilliam had warned her of this, but after the manner of most of the ladies they had called upon today, this lady was different in a marked way. The lady whom they visited at the moment more resembled Miss Bingley in the tone and nature of her tittle-tattle. How much longer would they remain? She had missed seeing Fitzwilliam for this?

"Miss Bennet!" Elizabeth perked up at the lady's booming address. What had Lady Albemarle been saying? Which son of a baronet married his mistress? "I am so pleased Lady Fitzwilliam has brought you to call today. I had heard rumours of Miss Bingley's disappointment." She waved her hand as if dismissing the hearsay. "Mind you, I never believed Mr. Darcy would offer for that woman. She should not have put all of her eggs in one basket. She is destined for the shelf, and her brother is now panicked he will be supporting her for the rest of his life—not that I blame him. I have seen her at the milliners. I would wager she spends more than her pin money allows—not that the gowns reflect their cost. The colours she chooses are dreadful."

Elizabeth's gaze flitted to Lady Fitzwilliam. She had warned Elizabeth there could be talk, but how much was being said? "I made the acquaintance of Miss Bingley when her brother leased the estate neighbouring my father's. I must admit to being unaware of Miss Bingley's hopes. We are not such intimate friends that she would share her most personal feelings."

"I daresay Miss Bingley told a great number of people her expectations," said Lady Albemarle with a hearty laugh. "She should not have been so confident without the gentleman providing her some encouragement. The entire *ton* knew he would not choose her. I must say I am happy to see he chose more of a lady." She dipped her chin and held up a finger, swaying it back and forth. "I would never call Miss Bingley a true lady."

Elizabeth struggled to keep a placid countenance. How could she speak so in front of someone she had just met? Well, she would not provide Lady Albemarle any more gossip than possible. "I cannot speak to Miss Bingley's behaviour or temper. When we were in company together, she spoke to her sister more than to me."

"Lady Albemarle, you know Mrs. Hurst, do you not?" asked Lady Fitzwilliam in her accented tone. Elizabeth had never heard a voice like hers before.

"I do! Those two ladies may as well have shared a womb, only Mrs. Hurst was willing to wed a man who awaited the inheritance of a modest estate. She kept her ambitions realistic, if you ask me."

Lady Fitzwilliam nodded. "I would have to agree. Did you hear Mr. Bingley made a scene yesterday at White's? He seems to think my nephew honour-bound to his sister. Can you imagine?"

"I had heard from my husband of the entire affair!" Lady Albemarle pressed her hand to her chest in a dramatic manner. "He was witness to the young man making the accusation as well as your son refuting it. The nerve of Mr. Bingley. Your nephew was too good to befriend him, but he must see what damage can be wrought by befriending a tradesman."

Lady Fitzwilliam gave a barely perceptible shake of her head to Elizabeth before she peered over her shoulder at the clock. "Oh! Do look at the time! Forgive me, but I promised Miss Bennet's aunt and uncle I would have her home before dinner." She stood and cupped her hand around her mouth. "I also wanted to bring her by Darcy House for a quick cup of tea with my nephew and niece. I am sure you understand."

"I certainly do." Lady Albemarle hoisted her generous frame from the settee and dipped a slight curtsey. "Thank you for calling and bringing Miss Bennet. I am thrilled beyond measure to have met the lady. I can now claim to any who may be giving credit to the Bingleys' lies that Miss Bennet is every bit a true lady—unlike some." She lowered her voice when she said the last, giving no doubt to who she referred.

"Thank you," said Elizabeth as she returned the curtsey. She fiddled with the ribbons of her reticule while Lady Fitzwilliam bade Lady Albemarle farewell.

As soon as they were seated inside the carriage, Lady Fitzwilliam loosened her bonnet as she relaxed into the seat. "I apologise for Lady Albemarle. I confess she was nothing more than strategy."

"You are not friends then?" Elizabeth's initial sketch of Lady Albemarle was not favourable, and Lady Fitzwilliam was not one to suffer fools gladly. If they were friends, how did she bear the association?

"That is a complicated question. Lady Albemarle was a dear friend and confidante when we were young. We attended the same school and came out during the same season. She did enjoy gossip, but not as she does now. She was never blessed with children, and I have watched her with each year become more and more interested in the lives of others. Her alteration is a result of dissatisfaction and unhappiness, so I have never turned my back on her." Lady Fitzwilliam sighed and glanced out of the window. "We are not as close as we once were, but I do still call on her regularly. For today's purposes, this was a strategic visit. We needed her sanction and her propensity to talk to whomever crosses her path."

Elizabeth sagged into the squabs and blew out a ragged breath. "Forgive me. I do appreciate all you are doing. I simply find it trying and rather exhausting."

Lady Fitzwilliam bent forward and patted her knee. "I do understand, but we cannot let Miss Bingley and her brother discredit you or pursue this ridiculous attempt to force Fitzwilliam's hand. If you noticed, the gossip was mentioned during each and every call we made today. Having them see you and witness your genteel behaviour was vital."

"I may be a gentleman's daughter, but I still have connections to trade. You heard Lady Albemarle speak of the Bingleys."

"But you are a gentleman's daughter. Of course, your lack of fortune as well as the connection to your aunt and uncle will be mentioned, and some may snub you, but those families would reject the Bingleys as well. Those two have been tolerated for no other reason than the brother's friendship with Fitzwilliam. Miss Bingley believes she is well liked when most of society despises her. Mrs. Hurst would be better accepted if she did not follow her sister's lead."

"Yet they admit them to their drawing rooms." Was she the only one who saw the hypocrisy?

The lady's lips curved a little. "I understand what you are saying, but I suppose I perceive the situation differently. My husband likes to quote a book he brought back from France during his Grand Tour. 'Keep your friends close and your enemies closer' is the saying."

With a frown, Elizabeth's head hitched back a bit. "What book is this?"

Lady Fitzwilliam gave a dismissive wave of her hand. "Oh, I do not know what it is called. He has said it was translated to French from ancient Chinese. If you wish to know, ask him when you meet him, but be warned, he can drone on and on about that ridiculous thing for ages." She tapped her fingers upon the seat beside her. "I must know that you understand what I am saying in regard to Miss Bingley."

"I believe so," said Elizabeth. "They do not like her, but they admit her to be aware of what she says and perhaps use her to their advantage."

"Precisely!" Lady Fitzwilliam's unusual accent thickened with the definitive tone of voice.

"I am not sure that is better." Elizabeth rubbed her forehead. That slight throbbing behind her eyes was intensifying. "I avoided Miss Bingley in Meryton because I found her disagreeable. I have no care what she says about me. I understand wishing to suppress damage to Fitzwilliam, but I would prefer to forget the lady exists."

"Then let me be of aid," said Lady Fitzwilliam. "Once we have managed this situation, you may do as you wish. I simply want to keep Miss Bingley's machinations where they belong—

in her own mind and not intruding upon the equanimity of Fitzwilliam and Georgiana. I hope you can understand my motives." The carriage stuttered to a halt, and the lady peered through the window. "Ah, here we are."

When Elizabeth followed Lady Fitzwilliam's line of sight, she laughed. "You were in earnest. I thought you were making an excuse."

"I do try not to lie, my dear. If you noticed during the calls, I did not speak much with the exception of stating fact: you are being courted by Fitzwilliam, Miss Bingley knew you in Hertfordshire, and Miss Bingley is jealous you succeeded where she failed. Whatever else was said about the lady was the opinions and assumptions of others."

The door opened, and Lady Fitzwilliam alighted with Elizabeth following. Watson ushered them inside at the same time as Fitzwilliam opened his study door, a beautiful grin upon his features. "What a wonderful surprise! I had not known you would call."

"Where is Georgiana?" asked Lady Fitzwilliam while she removed her gloves. "I desire a word with her." She peered back and forth between them. "Fitzwilliam, I trust you will return her to Gracechurch Street?"

He gave a slight twitch, then offered an eager nod. "Of course. I shall be pleased to do so."

His aunt bustled towards the ponderous notes of the pianoforte in the music room while Elizabeth leaned back against the wall. "Must I do that again?"

His warm laugh soothed her frayed nerves. "I am almost afraid to ask where you called today."

She pressed her palm to her forehead. "I do not remember all of the names. I fear I am hopeless in that regard, but I can tell you the last was Lady Albemarle."

His nose wrinkled. "I am familiar with the lady." He stepped closer and took her hand. "Was my aunt's quest successful?"

"Quest?" She laughed and straightened as he kissed her knuckles, sending a torrent of flutterings through her. "You make her sound as if she were hunting for hidden treasure or joining the crusades, though I believe today's goal may have been as harrowing as the crusades." She pressed the fingers of her free hand to her temple.

"Does your head pain you?" He rubbed his thumb against the palm of the hand he still held in his grasp. Did he not know how difficult it was to speak when he did that?

"A little," she said.

"Come." He tugged her into his study, steered her to the sofa which stood before the fire, then handed her a measured glass of sherry. "Drink this. I could request laudanum from Mrs. Northcott—"

"Laudanum? Do you mean to have me fall asleep?" She lifted her eyebrow. "Do you not know 'tis difficult as it is to think in your presence—" No! She clapped her hand over her mouth.

He tugged her arm away, wearing, if possible, an even wider grin. "Do not fret. I feel the same at times." He took the seat beside her and laced their fingers together. "I am sorry for this. I have told Bingley for years I would never marry his sister. I implored him to tell her so as well. Her attentions and the implied intimacy of some of her statements frustrated me. I never expected that when I found a lady to court, he would behave so."

"I do not blame you." She relaxed and looked down to stare at their entwined fingers. "After his behaviour with Jane, I have come to believe he has no real convictions or empathy. His unwillingness to stand up to his sister as well as his ultimatum demonstrate his selfish disdain for your feelings. I remember your manner with Miss Bingley at Netherfield." Miss Bingley's offer to mend Fitzwilliam's pen came to mind. How could she have not noticed Miss Bingley's partiality for him then? "You offered her no encouragement. You were barely more civil to her than you were to me."

He closed his eyes and dropped his head. "If you only knew how much I wish I could change—"

"No," she said, releasing her hand to make him lift his gaze and meet hers. She smiled in an attempt to soothe him. "Do not make yourself uneasy. I was attempting to tease you, but the pain in my head may be interfering with my wit." She squeezed his hand. "You must think only of the past as its remembrance gives you pleasure. I believe we have started anew, have we not?"

"I should say we have."

"Then, we shall not speak of this again unless it is with fondness. I no longer bear you a grudge for your comments. I have learnt to laugh at them, particularly now that I know they were falsehoods."

He trailed a finger from her temple to her chin. "As long as I have changed your opinion of me, I shall be satisfied."

"Your aunt is a unique lady," said Elizabeth, resting her elbow on the back of the sofa. "I do not believe I have ever heard an accent like hers. Her complexion is lovely but not English. I have tried to discern where she is from, but I cannot place it."

"My aunt was born in Portugal to a Portuguese mother and English father. After her mother's death, her father, who was an earl, returned to England where she attended school and eventually wed my uncle. Their marriage is a love match, but he was quite envied to have caught her the year she came out."

"Why is that?"

"Because she is a distant cousin to Queen Charlotte through a member of the Portuguese royal family named Margarita de Castro y Sousa." The entire time Fitzwilliam spoke, he toyed with her fingers and softly stroked her knuckles. He made it difficult to think.

"I do not believe I have ever seen an image of the queen. Do they favour one another at all?"

"They share a few features," he said. "The mother of Margarita's husband was the Moorish mistress of King Alfonso of Portugal. A few have claimed her features unfashionable, but they are rare since to insult my aunt's complexion is to insult that of the queen's."

"Indeed."

"I do not mean to belittle my aunt, but I would prefer to discuss anything but her and the *ton*." His palm cradled her cheek, and her heart began to pound in her chest. She shivered as his face crept closer and closer. Would he kiss her as he had on Christmas day? His lips met hers and she gripped her skirts while his lips slid along hers in a slightly different manner than under the kissing bough. Her skin prickled and her trembling increased, spurred by the warmth of his breath as it caressed her cheek. How did one not expire from such sensations? A sudden giggle made her jerk away and cover her mouth.

"Aunt!" said Georgiana in a dramatic whisper worthy of Elizabeth's mother. "He is kissing her!"

Fitzwilliam's head dropped to her shoulder. "Would that I could without someone announcing it?"

Elizabeth bit her lip. He was rather adorable when he pouted.

Chapter 14

Darcy covered his nose with his handkerchief in an attempt to avoid the putrid odour of the air while he alighted the carriage and waited for his uncle and Richard to join him. Before him, the façade of his gentlemen's club loomed. Lord, but he had no desire to go inside! Why had Bingley become all that Darcy despised about society? Too many who thought entirely too well of themselves, as well as those who desired to be more than they were—like Bingley. Those, who in their desperation to elevate their status, became no more than a squirrel clinging with as much strength as it could muster onto that lowest limb. Bingley had made a jump for a branch somewhere in the middle. The fall would be a painful one.

"Well? Are you prepared for this?" asked his uncle with a hand to Darcy's shoulder.

"I am astounded that you had his membership revoked so quickly." While Darcy had sponsored Bingley, he had not been able to bring himself to do the younger man harm, not that this caused a physical injury, but the impact would certainly be a personal affront.

"I knew you would not do so, and, thus, it was up to me. In some ways, you resemble your father more than you are aware. Your father coddled Wickham out of loyalty to his steward and friend and look what a reprobate the man became. I have no doubt, if left to you, you would have let things stand due to your former friendship. I assure you that Bingley will take advantage of your perceived weakness."

He glanced between his cousin and his uncle. "And what makes you think he will come today?"

His cousin snickered. "The puppy is a creature of habit. He always comes on Wednesdays." He waved them towards the entrance. "Let us go in. I have no desire to await him outside."

Lord Fitzwilliam led the way through the door and peered over his shoulder. "You did that boy an incredible favour by sponsoring him. If you recall, I never thought he would be admitted, and a good number of the peerage were not pleased at his entrance."

"I do remember," said Darcy as they entered the ground floor morning room. They sat in comfortable chairs in the corner nearest the window overlooking St. James Street, but he could not appreciate the supple leather nor the cushion of the seat. His shoulders were strung tight, and he pulled them forward and back in an effort to release the tension. He despised this.

"Say, Darcy!" They turned and stood at the sight of Lord Albemarle, who made his way over with a crooked grin upon his countenance. "I just saw your wife calling at my house."

"I beg your pardon?" Was Lord Albemarle confused? "The lady I am courting, Miss Elizabeth Bennet, joined Lady Fitzwilliam in a call upon your wife two days ago. We have not yet wed."

The wire-thin earl snickered and scratched his generous sideburns. "No, I mean this morning. That woman who always claims a connection to you..." He frowned before his face brightened. "Miss Bingley! That is her name. She arrived as I departed with that sister of hers, the one with the ginger hair. I distinctly heard her provide the name 'Mrs. Darcy' to my butler."

His teeth ground against each other with enough force to cause pain in his temples. "She is trying to entrap me."

"But Mother took Miss Elizabeth to Lady Albemarle's," said Richard, his foot tapping in an incessant rhythm upon the dark wood floor. "Lady Albemarle should be well aware of the truth of the matter."

His uncle stood. "I shall go upstairs and pen a message to my wife. She will never forgive me if I did not send word with the utmost haste."

"I shall join you," said Albemarle. "Are you gents not going up for a drink?"

"No, they are awaiting the brother, Bingley." Lord Fitzwilliam tugged at his waistcoat. "The addlepate's membership has been revoked."

"Capital! Bingley should have never been a member in the first place. I have always believed those in trade should be landed for at least three generations before they are considered gentry. That vulgar behaviour would be trained out of them by then." Albemarle followed Lord Fitzwilliam, holding up a hand behind him as he looked over his shoulder. "Good luck, Darcy."

"That bunter," said Richard in a growl. "I knew she was artful, but this is beyond the pale. I wonder if we can bring some sort of legal case against Bingley or even his sister. Perhaps we can have her sent to Bedlam?" He shook his head. "You need to wed Miss Elizabeth, and soon. What if Bingley brings a case for breach of promise?"

Darcy dropped his head into his hands and pulled at his hair until it stung. "I do not know, Richard, but I shall not rush Miss Elizabeth to accept me before she is ready."

"If my mother is to be believed, you have kissed her. You should not have even been alone with her."

"I know, though the door was open." He looked up and fisted his hand upon the table in front of him. "Elizabeth seems willing, but I do not want this cloud hanging over the memory of our wedding."

His cousin huffed. "Then you may pay the ultimate price for your recalcitrance."

At a flash of ginger-blond curls, Darcy's attention jerked to the window where Bingley strode with a liveliness to his step towards the entrance. "He is here."

Richard sprang from his chair and hastened towards the hall while Darcy hurried to catch up. As they neared the front, a sound Darcy had never heard before echoed through the room. Was that Bingley yelling?

"What do you mean my membership has been revoked? There must be some mistake!"

His cousin grabbed his arm, and they slowed as they approached. Darcy stood tall and steeled himself to maintain an implacable countenance. If only he could do so without conscious thought!

Bingley's face was pale when they stepped closer but recovered as he turned a remarkable shade of crimson. "You! You had my membership revoked?"

"If you remember, Bingley, I sponsored you. I had thought you my friend and wanted to help you become established and a landowner. Your unwillingness to control your sister's lies and machinations as well as your insistence now that I am honour-bound to her gave me no choice. I shall not be trapped in a marriage to Miss Bingley, regardless of what that does to my reputation."

"How—"

"Have you seen your sister this morning?" said Richard in a low and dangerous tone. "Lord Albemarle told us she is making calls under the name 'Mrs. Darcy.' Has she finally begun to believe her delusions? I believe that is called Spinster's Hysteria, is it not? Perhaps we should seek legal advice. I am certain Bedlam would have a bed for such a poor soul."

"You would not dare," said Bingley, his eyes narrowing.

Darcy took two steps forward, causing Bingley to take a step back. "Why should we not? I am also curious how much of this Hurst knows. His father still controls his inheritance. What would he think of your sister's antics—of his wife's antics? According to Lord Albemarle, Mrs. Hurst accompanied her sister." The younger man opened his mouth several times in succession before it snapped closed, then Bingley pivoted on his heel and made a swift exit.

"I always thought he was a coward." They both turned as Lord Fitzwilliam strode up behind them. "I take it he was not pleased."

"Not in the least," said Richard. "But I believe Darcy had a brilliant idea after I threatened to send Miss Bingley to Bedlam with Spinster's Hysteria."

The earl laughed under his breath. "I had not considered such a plan, but it does have merit. What was also said?"

Darcy shrugged and pinched the top of his nose. Lord, but this was making his head throb. "What if we confront Hurst? His wife was with Miss Bingley on her call this morning.

Could her sanction of Miss Bingley's behaviour damage his prospects?"

His uncle wagged his finger in Darcy's direction. "I have met the elder Mr. Hurst. He is a right tyrant and exceedingly aware of his family's reputation. I do believe his club is Boodle's, which would mean his son is likely a member as well." They stepped outside and the earl waved them to follow. "Perhaps fortune may shine upon us, and I shall manage to procure us an audience with the son."

Lord Fitzwilliam spoke to the man at the door, and somehow had them admitted to the members' suites where they took a look around until they spotted Hurst sitting in a corner with two older men. The trio drank brandy and chuckled about something or another. Darcy had never seen him so alive.

His cousin pushed him. "Well?"

He glanced back to his uncle, nodding, then took several steps until he stood beside the grouping. "Pardon me, but I need to speak to you, Hurst, if you have a moment."

The man looked up and swayed. Could the man be in his cups before noon? Was he ever lucid? "Whatever do you need?" His manner was brusque. What if this went poorly?

"I believe you would wish to have this conversation in private." Darcy, after all, would desire a conversation such as this without an audience.

With a noisy exhale, Hurst drew himself out of the chair. "Very well." As soon as they were away from prying ears, the man turned and crossed his arms over his chest. "Now, what is this about?"

"Are you aware Bingley is attempting to force my hand with Miss Bingley? He has claimed I am honour bound."

Hurst blinked several times and frowned. "What sort of balderdash is he playing at? Is he addled?"

Darcy pressed his lips together to keep from laughing. "I am unsure of his motives, but this morning, Lord Albemarle claimed Miss Bingley called upon his wife, giving the name 'Mrs. Darcy' to the butler."

The shorter man furrowed his brow and rubbed his forehead. "Bloody hell! The news of your attendance at the theatre and the subsequent knowledge of Miss Elizabeth's identity as the lady you are courting is common knowledge. I learnt of that here at the club. What can Caroline possibly hope to accomplish?"

"I believe she is hoping to increase the likelihood of forcing me into a marriage. Angry people are rarely wise." He exhaled heavily. "As a result, Bingley's membership to White's has been revoked."

Hurst gave a small bark of laughter. "Forgive me, but he never belonged there. I was amazed he was ever given admittance."

"My uncle and cousin are urging me to consult my solicitor about having Miss Bingley committed to Bedlam. As I am not a relation, I am unsure if I am able to do so, but she is not right."

Hurst held up a finger, walked over to where he had been sitting, downed his brandy, and walked back. "I needed the fortification. Now, what do you desire from me?"

Darcy winced and held his hands, palm out, in front of him. "I would never ask you to act against your own family, but I thought you should be informed."

Hurst's eyes flared for a second before he sighed. "I thank you for the consideration. I am unsure of what to do, but I will consult with my father. He would be quite displeased to know what Caroline is up to." He wagged his finger in front of him. "You know Caroline's dinner was last night, and I thought it peculiar you did not attend. Of course, now that I know this..."

"I had responded that I would attend, but I would be surprised if she expected me after what has occurred. As to your family, you must do as you see fit."

Hurst held out a hand. "As do you. I appreciate your warning." After they shook hands, Darcy bowed and returned to his uncle.

"Well?" asked Lord Fitzwilliam.

"He had no idea. He asked what I wanted of him but never proposed to be of aid, not that I expected him to. I would never ask him to work against his own family."

"But would that not be a coup if he offered?" said Richard. "I do not know about you, but I have had enough of gentlemen's clubs for the day. Shall we return to Wentworth House for luncheon? Mother said she invited Miss Elizabeth as well as Georgiana."

Elizabeth would be at his aunt's? Her company would be sure to settle him, thus he required no further invitation.

Chapter 15

The quiet pathway of the park stretched out before them as they made a circuit of the lake, Elizabeth's hand nestled in the crook of Fitzwilliam's arm. After the fantastic happenings with Miss Bingley, she welcomed the peace of the prospect. The bare branches of the elms contrasted not only with the plane trees with their dead leaves still hanging on despite the cold but also with the verdant green of the mistletoe clinging to many of the branches.

His hand covered hers in a way she had come to expect and adore. "What are you thinking?"

"I believe I am attempting not to think and fret." As soon as they had departed the house, he had not only told her of what had occurred at his club but also of his conversation with Mr. Hurst. Who knew that man could do more than laze upon the sofa and snore?

"Do you believe Mr. Hurst will be of aid to us?"

"I am inclined to believe he will. He has a younger brother. If his father feels Mrs. Hurst is harming the family's reputation, Mr. Hurst could lose his inheritance to his sibling."

She winced and shook her head. "I am sorry for him. I do not know why he wed Mrs. Hurst, but to have his future at stake due to her actions is careless on her part. What have your uncle and your cousin to say of the matter?"

He made a sudden stop and turned to face her. "My uncle is furious with Bingley. I am still amazed at the swiftness of his expulsion from my club. As for Richard, he believes we should wed with haste."

"He believes Miss Bingley's plot will succeed?" She could not help the incredulity in her voice. How could such a blatant abuse of societal rules succeed? How unfair would that be to Fitzwilliam? She pressed her free palm to her stomach in a futile attempt to quell her nerves. Was this what Fitzwilliam wished?

"No," he said, "but he would prefer to quash any scheme of hers whether he thinks it has a possibility of succeeding or not. If we were wed, the rumours would still abound for a time, but Bingley would have no chance of recourse."

"He could sue for breach of promise, could he not?"

"We never had an understanding, and I am uncertain if he could convince a judge to his or his sister's view."

She kept her breathing even and steady while her heart thudded in a heavy beat. "What do you want? Do you wish for a hurried affair?"

He took her hands in his and held them between them. "While I want nothing more than you as my bride, I would not have you rushed or uncomfortable. I do not want you to regret the method of our betrothal or wedding."

"Jane laments ever believing him a gentleman, or his sister amiable." She sighed and released his hands, taking a couple of steps towards the pond's edge. "My feelings are so different from when you left Hertfordshire. The swiftness of my attachment to you frightens me at times."

He gave a slight gasp. "I frighten you?"

"No," she said, facing him. "I suppose I thought when I fell in love, my affection would strengthen and deepen over time, becoming fuller over months. I did not expect you." One side of her lips tugged upwards. "You stepped into my days and overwhelmed. I once thought you the last man in the world I could be prevailed upon to marry, but now..."

His eyebrows shot up. "But now?" He swallowed hard, his Adam's apple bobbing.

How could she say this? Would he think her brazen or wanton? She took in a deep breath and crossed her arms over her chest. "Now, you are the only man I could be prevailed upon to marry."

He stepped forward but halted and glanced over his shoulder at the footman who stood watch, though the servant was not so close as to hear their conversation. He drew her gloved hands away from her body with care not to be overly familiar and once again held them in a delicate grip. "I do love you, Elizabeth. I hope I am not speaking to soon."

Elizabeth lifted her one eyebrow. "I have let you kiss me, sir. I believe speaking of what that means is long overdue, do you not agree?"

He smiled with a wide, open countenance that made him appear much younger than was his wont. "So, since you do not object to my saying 'I love you,' may I enquire as to your feelings?"

She squeezed his hands and attempted to steady herself. Why did she seem to be in a near constant state of dizziness when he was around? "I never expected to love you," she said with a bit of a laugh. "But, I do find myself loving you a bit more every day. What can I do when you have stolen my heart right out from under my very nose?"

He lifted her hands to his lips and dropped to his knee. "Then I must ask, Elizabeth Bennet, will you do me the honour of marrying me? I have loved you since I first saw you laugh at that horrid assembly. I promise to do all in my power to make you happy for the rest of our lives."

She rolled her eyes with a grin and shrugged. "Well, I suppose I must agree. What else could I do when I find I love you too?"

"Is that a 'yes'?"

"Yes," she said laughing. "Yes, now stand up, you silly, perfectly wonderful man, before you ruin your breeches."

After he rose, he ran his fingers through his hair. "We can plan a wedding to take place in a month or so if you wish. Do not feel we must commit to an immediate ceremony because my cousin feels it would be prudent."

"I would be content with your cousin's scheme. Pray, do not believe me terrible, but I would prefer to avoid Mama's planning, not to mention the dinners and teas she would insist upon. The ceremony means little to me in comparison to the life that will come after. If we can cease whatever scheme Mr. Bingley and Miss Bingley are attempting in the process, I shall not complain."

He blinked rapidly and tilted his head. "I need to speak to your uncle, then your father."

"Perhaps I should write my father and summon him here? He was not pleased about our courtship, but only as he could not speak to me of how my feelings have altered. I penned him a letter in response. He has not answered." She tugged him back along the pathway, and her hand returned to the crook of his arm.

"Do you believe he will object?"

"I do not think so. If he were to refuse his consent, Mama would never forgive him." She rubbed her palm against her stomach in an attempt to soothe those butterflies. She had said yes! She did not regret her acceptance. Those butterflies never failed to appear during these sorts of moments. How was it possible her skin seemed the only thing keeping her from bursting into a thousand pieces?

"My aunt's Twelfth Night ball is in five days, and regardless of the excuse, my aunt will insist upon my attendance. What if I applied for a special license? I am certain my uncle could ensure I receive one without delay, then we could wed in the drawing room at Darcy House. If we can arrange the ceremony before long, then we have a day or so to ourselves before attending the ball as a married couple. My aunt would be ecstatic to introduce us. After, we could remain for the Season, or we could remove to Pemberley and avoid the experience altogether."

She smiled and nudged him with her elbow. "You do detest balls and society with a vengeance, do you not?"

"Perhaps I am being stingy. I do not want to share you when I finally have you all to myself."

She feigned a gasp. "And what of your poor sister? Are we to abandon her to the whims of her companion?"

"No," he said, "She would stay with my aunt for a time. I would suggest a wedding trip to the Lakes or the seaside, but those would be better suited to late spring or the summer months."

"My aunt and uncle are planning a journey to the Lakes this summer. I was supposed to travel with them, but perhaps they will take Jane in my stead."

They left through the gate of the park and continued towards her uncle's house. "They could break their journey at Pemberley. Perhaps I shall be willing to share you by then."

"Who knew I would marry such a selfish man?"

His deep rumble of a laugh echoed along the street. "Only when it comes to you."

When they entered the house, Fitzwilliam knocked upon her uncle's door, but his eyes never left hers until he stepped inside. Once the door closed, she made her way into the parlour and sat in her usual place, picking up her needlework before setting it in her lap and pressing her palms to her cheeks. She could not cease grinning.

"Did you walk around the pond?"

Her head jerked up to her aunt. "Yes, the weather has a slight chill, but no breeze, so it was bearable."

Aunt Gardiner's eyes narrowed. "You are flushed. Are you certain you are not falling ill?"

"I am well, thank you."

"Lizzy, you almost cannot sit still," said Jane. "Whatever has caused this?"

Her aunt gasped and covered her mouth with her hands. "He asked, did he not?"

"What?" Jane jumped up and hurried over to stare down at Elizabeth. "Well? Did he?"

Elizabeth bit her lip and nodded before she was pulled up from the chair and wrapped in her aunt's embrace. "Dear girl, I am so pleased for you. He is such a good man, and he loves you." She pulled back. "I can tell by the way he looks at you."

After Jane hugged her, Elizabeth covered her cheeks once more. "I cannot stop smiling."

"And why should you?" Her aunt took her hands. "We should make you an appointment with Madame de Beaulieu for your wedding clothes."

Elizabeth sucked a small amount of air between her teeth. "I am afraid if my uncle is agreeable, I may not have sufficient time."

"Whatever do you mean?" asked her aunt with wide eyes.

"Merely that Mr. Darcy and I do not want the usual affair. He plans to acquire a special license. We thought to wed before his aunt's ball on Twelfth Night."

Jane propped her hands upon her hips. "Is this because of Mr. Bingley and his sister?"

"A little, but we also do not want to wait. I do not mean to sound terrible, Jane, but I cannot allow Mama to plan dinners and dances and parade me around to the neighbours as though I am her prize sow."

Her aunt laughed and pressed her hand over her mouth before letting it drop. "I am certain it will not be so bad."

"I admit to feeling the same dread when I thought Mr. Bingley might propose," said Jane. "I do not blame you."

The door opened, and her uncle entered. "Lizzy, Mr. Darcy desires a word before he departs. Have you told them your news?"

"Yes, Uncle."

He kissed her cheek. "Congratulations, my dear. You have made a spectacular match. When your mother learns the news, I am certain we shall hear her raptures from here." He grinned at his own foolishness. "Now, go. Your betrothed awaits you in my study."

She hastened from the parlour into the study. When she entered, Fitzwilliam stretched out an arm, taking her hand and tugging her closer until he pressed his lips to hers. "You have made me so happy today," he said when he began to straighten.

Without thinking, she rose onto her tiptoes and bestowed the kiss this time. His arm wound around her middle and she leaned against him as the kiss changed, and he teased her lips apart. His tongue caressed hers, and her heart was about burst from her chest.

His hands clenched at the back of her gown while he claimed more and more of her. He groaned, then suddenly withdrew. "Forgive me. I forgot myself."

"If you did, then I provoked you to it."

He smiled and drew her back into his embrace, touching his forehead to hers. "Your uncle will pen a letter to go with yours. He is of the same mind as my cousin: that we should be wed as soon as may be. If Bingley attempts a legal case, he does not want you abandoned. Your reputation as well as that of your sisters would suffer."

"I had not considered..." She cared not of Miss Bingley. Impulsivity was never an attribute she could claim, but when she considered the possibility of losing Fitzwilliam, she could not bear it. He was hers. Now, she merely wanted her life with him to begin.

"No need to be concerned. I am off to Wentworth House, then to Doctors' Commons."

"When shall I see you next?"

"Tomorrow, I shall come tomorrow. I promise."

Her fingers combed through his soft, dark curls. "Kiss me again."

His jaw clenched and released. "I fear if I begin, I shall not stop. You are too tempting, my love."

His lips pressed against her forehead, and before she could persuade him to more, he was gone.

Chapter 16

"I beg your pardon, Mr. Darcy."

He spun around from his vigil before the window to Mrs. Hendricks, who stood in the door of his study. "Yes, come in. Is there a problem?" If all went as it should, he would be wed and wed soon to Elizabeth, and he was a wreck. His valet had him dressed this morning in his best suit, but not without a few pursed lips and exhales at the younger man's fit of nerves. Thankfully, his nerves did not plague him often!

"No, sir. All should be prepared. Cook has made a cake and punch and will have a small breakfast for the guests." He nodded, though if asked, he could not have repeated a word of what she said. "Miss Elizabeth's trunks were delivered a short time ago."

He perked up and joined his hands behind his back. "Good," he said. Had he sounded calm? He had attempted to temper the burst from within when his housekeeper imparted that important morsel of news. "Forgive me, Mrs. Hendricks, but I am not certain I understand why you have need of me."

"I suppose I should be more direct." She moved further into the room. "Miss Bennet's trunks arrived, but no maid accompanied them. Does she have an abigail?"

Georgiana hurried in and grabbed his arm. "I cannot wait for Elizabeth to arrive." She glanced back and forth between them. "Is aught amiss?"

"Do you know if Elizabeth has a maid of her own?"

His sister frowned and ceased bouncing on her toes. "I do not think so. She mentioned that at Longbourn, she and her sisters shared a maid. I believe Mrs. Gardiner has a girl who helps Elizabeth and Jane, but she is Mrs. Gardiner's servant."

He scratched the back of his neck. "Mrs. Hendricks, pray, set a few of the maids to work putting away Miss Elizabeth's belongings."

"We should ask our aunt when she arrives," said Georgiana. "She may know of someone."

"Excellent thought, Poppet."

When he turned back to the window, the Gardiner's carriage stood at the kerb, and he rushed into the hall as Watson opened the door. As soon as Mr. Gardiner entered, he bowed and slapped Darcy on the shoulder. "My sister would not let Elizabeth be this morning, so we insisted she ride with us in our carriage. The Bennets should not be far behind us. Do you have a spare room where we might hide your intended until the vicar arrives?" The twinkle in Mr. Gardiner's eye spoke of his good humour in the situation, but his attention was arrested by the sight of Elizabeth as she approached.

She held both Mrs. Gardiner's and Miss Bennet's arms, which she released once they stood face to face. He could not remove his gaze from her sparkling eyes to her ebony curls peeking from the edges of her pearl-coloured bonnet. When she removed her blush pelisse, her pearl silk gown was trimmed with pale blue embroidery and a matching ribbon around her waistline.

He offered her his arm as another equipage arrived in front of the house. "I believe you require sanctuary."

His heart swelled as her small hand wrapped around his elbow. "I have desired to take my embroidery needle and stitch Mama's mouth closed this morning. She has been dreadful, and

Papa finds the greatest amusement in it all. She believes Lydia should remain with us after the ceremony, so we can introduce her to rich men during the Season."

He blanched. "What did you tell her?"

"I said I was unsure if we would remain in London, and that you had mentioned a strong desire to forgo the Season and return to your estate. I am afraid she was horrified by the notion. Expect her to make an attempt to persuade you otherwise."

Once he was assured Elizabeth was comfortable in the music room, he followed the sound of bellowing back to the hall. Blast! Why was his aunt in London?

"I will see my nephew!" As soon as Lady Catherine noticed him, she lifted her walking stick. "Ah! There you are. I have heard you are courting a most unsuitable lady, and I have come to ensure you honour your mother's dying wish—to marry Anne."

He cringed and suppressed the shudder that threatened to wrack his spine. His aunt had been reciting that same story for a decade at least. "Lady Catherine, if you will join me in my study, we can discuss what you have been told."

She shoved Watson to the side with some force, the older man stumbling out of his aunt's path. "I am here for no other reason than to see you do your duty. I shall not be dissuaded."

With the door closed behind him, he stood with his back against the solid oak panel. "Aunt, I am not certain what gossip you have heard—"

"I received this yesterday," she said proffering a folded piece of parchment. "Upon perusing its foul message, I made haste to town to see its claims contradicted."

He made quick work of reading the heavily slanted writing contained in the missive. He was at no loss as to who penned the correspondence. Miss Bingley had a distinct penmanship. "You would take the word of a tradesman's daughter who is conspiring to force my hand."

His aunt's head jerked back. "The letter is unsigned. How do you know who wrote it?"

"Bingley and I first met at Eton and later crossed paths at Cambridge before becoming friends. He and his sister often exchanged letters during school. I have seen her handwriting on more than one occasion since he sometimes read her correspondence with me present." He then explained Miss Bingley's current scheme without mentioning Elizabeth or their courtship and subsequent betrothal. If he could persuade his aunt to depart, he could notify her by correspondence of his nuptials. He simply wanted her to leave as quickly as possible. He had a wedding to attend.

"That harlot!" His aunt pounded her walking stick against the floor upon his explanation. Hopefully, she did not mar the wood. She once left a dent in the floor of Rosings, so it would not be a singular event. "Where can I find this woman? I must insist she cease her useless machinations immediately."

"Of course, Aunt. If you could convince her of the futility of her scheme, I would be grateful indeed." Would that she could!

His aunt sucked in a breath, pursed her lips, and nodded as soon as he gave her the direction. "I shall make haste. I know how to act!" She held the bit of parchment aloft. "I expect you at Rosings for Easter. We shall make the arrangements for your wedding to Anne."

"I have no desire to wed my cousin, Aunt, as she has no desire to marry me."

"The two of you have no idea what you are about, but we shall discuss that when you visit. In the meantime, I shall take care of this Miss Bingley." Before he could say another word, she was gone.

His uncle entered no more than a minute after his aunt departed. "I am afraid to ask where my sister is going with such haste."

"She intends to call upon Miss Bingley and insist the woman cease her pursuit of me." Darcy snickered under his breath. "I cannot imagine her succeeding, but I just thought of Miss Bingley's probable complexion at my aunt's rebuke."

Lord Fitzwilliam gave a hearty chuckle. "If it would not require keeping company with Catherine, I may have joined her in the endeavour." The siblings had never been close, so his uncle's willingness to accompany his sister was a rare idea indeed. "Now, let us get you wed before my sister returns. She will be none too pleased when she learns of this."

Darcy sighed. "Perhaps I can convince Elizabeth to take a wedding trip after all."

His uncle's chuckle boomed through the entry hall. "I meant to tell you. The clergyman and the Bennets have arrived. When you are ready to proceed, all is in waiting."

"Then let us not tarry. I am ready to claim my bride." And he was. Between the unexpected appearance of his aunt to the possibility of Miss Bingley arriving as a result of his aunt's call, he would not delay. "Watson," he said to the butler who stood near the entrance of the drawing room, "pray, tell the ladies in the music room that we are ready, and aside from Colonel

Fitzwilliam, no one is to be admitted—no one. Do you understand?"

"Yes, sir." The butler glanced at the earl. "Though you should know the colonel arrived with Lord and Lady Fitzwilliam. He awaits you in the drawing room." With a bow, he bustled away.

"Richard heard Catherine and was more than willing to let me fetch you."

Darcy rolled his eyes. His cousin had always been a coward when it came to his aunt. "I do not suppose Mrs. Bennet is quiet."

"Is that the lady who is appraising every piece of furniture and counting the windows?" His uncle slapped him on the back. "We made the acquaintance of the Bennets just before I came to get you."

When he entered, his aunt's lips were pursed, Mrs. Bennet's face was red, and Mr. Bennet's shoulders shook with laughter. Something had happened. Dare he ask what it was?

He was introduced to Mr. Brown, the vicar, before Mrs. Gardiner, Miss Bennet, and Elizabeth entered. He had seen her, of course, when she had first entered the house, but in that moment, he could have easily forgotten anyone else existed. She wore a tiny smile that caught him from the moment their eyes met and refused to let go.

His fingers twitched to touch her while Mr. Brown recited the ceremony. What would the poor man think if Darcy grabbed Elizabeth and crushed her to him in a passionate kiss? He stared at the curve of her shoulder, her small hand upon the arm of his top coat, and the line of her pert nose until someone cleared his throat. His intended laughed that happy sound that he would be content to drown in for the rest of his days. Wait! Why was she laughing?

When he returned his attention to the vicar, the man smiled while Elizabeth's upper arm pressed against his elbow. "You are supposed to answer 'I will,' Mr. Darcy," she said in a whisper near his shoulder.

"Yes, I will. Forgive me."

Elizabeth bit her lip, and he fought to keep from running his finger along the plump flesh and freeing it from her teeth. The imp was laughing at him. Her eyes sparkled and she peered up at him in such an alluring manner, he tensed to keep himself under regulation.

As soon as Mr. Brown pronounced them husband and wife, they signed the parish register before being surrounded by their families. His aunt kissed his cheek, and he grabbed her hand. "I need to ask you about a maid for—"

"Georgiana already mentioned Elizabeth's need for a lady's maid. I sent word to my housekeeper, who will send over the girl training under my abigail. She is excellent. If she suits, Mrs. Darcy may hire her for herself. Even so, she will have a maid while she searches for someone she prefers. Do let me know since I shall need to replace the maid should she remain with you."

"Thank you, Aunt."

"What would you do without me?" She patted his cheek before she stepped over to congratulate Elizabeth. When he had been slapped on the back by every man in the room and received the well-wishes of all the ladies, Mrs. Hendricks announced the breakfast.

While his aunt and uncle led the group into the dining room, Elizabeth leaned against his arm. "Do you think if we disappeared, anyone would notice?" He could not help but grin at the similarity in the turn of their minds. A part of him wanted to whisk her through the servants' passages to his rooms where they would be blessedly alone. How much longer until he could force their family to depart? He could do naught but count the minutes.

Chapter 17

By mid-afternoon, the Gardiners as well as Papa, eager for solitude and an end to his wife's unceasing nerves, had pressed a complaining Mama to join them on their return to Cheapside. Elizabeth had cringed at her mother's behaviour, which had devolved over the course of the day. Why could Mama not understand the impact of her poor manners?

"Now," said Lady Fitzwilliam as she took Elizabeth's wrist. "The two of you are not to venture out until my ball two days hence. We shall announce your marriage to all and sundry then. You must know I received a call from Miss Bingley and her brother yesterday—"

"What?" Fitzwilliam stiffened beside her. "Why would you not tell us this sooner? What business could they possibly have with you?"

Lord Fitzwilliam offered his wife his arm. "Your aunt refused to spoil your wedding by mentioning that family before the event."

"As for what they wanted, they hoped I could be convinced you were honour-bound to the sister. Lady Jersey called not five minutes after them, and upon her entrance, I invited them to the masquerade as an olive branch. I never told them you would make your debut as a married couple that evening, mind you, then had them escorted to the door. Once Lady Jersey departed, I made some calls and spoke of what happened. Those I spoke to are none too pleased with what those two are attempting." She patted Fitzwilliam's arm. "We shall discuss it further before the ball. I shall send a note as to what time you are to arrive." How could Lady Fitzwilliam be so at ease with all that had occurred? Elizabeth needed to swallow and take a deep breath to calm the nervousness arising in her chest.

Georgiana kissed both of their cheeks. "I am thrilled to call you sister, Elizabeth."

She jumped and returned her new sister's kisses. "As I am you," she said before the girl bounded out to the carriage. The Fitzwilliams followed, but Colonel Fitzwilliam paused and stared at the doorway. What could he possibly see that would make him behave so?

When they turned, Mr. Hurst stood upon the step. "Forgive me. I seem to be interrupting, but I have news of great import to you if you are inclined to hear it."

Fitzwilliam stepped forward and held out an arm. "Of course. Pray, come in."

His cousin waved the carriage away and closed the door. "If you have no objection, I shall join you."

"No objection at all, Cousin," said Fitzwilliam over his shoulder as he led them into the study.

As soon as the door closed, Mr. Hurst glanced around them then to Elizabeth's hand, held firmly in Fitzwilliam's. "I wish you joy, Mr. and Mrs. Darcy."

Her new husband pulled out the chair at his desk for her to sit. "We do not plan to make an announcement as yet. My aunt desires a grand audience at her ball."

The man held up a hand. "I shall not tell a soul—not even my wife." Mr. Hurst scratched the back of his neck and exhaled a weary breath. "After you departed my club, I hastened home. My wife and her sister were still making calls, and I was unsure of where Bingley had gone. With the house empty, I took the liberty of prying into my brother's affairs. You must know that after he let Netherfield, he withdrew substantial funds from his accounts. I also found an entry to the back of his account book, separate from his inheritance and business with additions and subtractions to the total sum. The withdrawals from his personal funds are subtracted from the sum in the back of the ledger. After puzzling over the numbers for some time, I noticed the specific days of the week of the entries."

The colonel laughed and shook his head. "I am going to hazard a guess they were the days he went to White's. I have seen him in the gambling rooms, but I thought naught of it at the time. He has amassed a substantial debt then?"

Mr. Hurst nodded and sighed while Fitzwilliam practically growled.

"Yes, he owes more than he possesses, even after the payments he has made," said Mr. Hurst. "He had in excess of £100,000 upon his father's death. He now has half that sum, and from what I can tell, Caroline's fortune is gone. She has nothing, and her expenses are a sieve to Bingley's coffers as well."

Her husband's fingers tightened upon her shoulder. Poor Fitzwilliam! What had been Mr. Bingley's ultimate goal? Had he wished for Fitzwilliam to pay his debts, or had he wanted nothing more than to rid himself of the expense of his sister? "With the sort of marriage Miss Bingley expects, how could her brother believe she would gain a husband without a fortune?"

"Elizabeth's observation has merit. Even Mrs. Darcy comes to me with a small portion—in her case, I do not begrudge the amount since she is worth far more to me than any money she could possess. But any man Miss Bingley considers suitable for marriage would desire at least £20,000."

His cousin crossed his arms over his chest. "He likely hoped Darcy would overlook the missing money or would even provide funds to eliminate his debt."

"No," said Fitzwilliam in a firm tone. "I learnt my lesson with Wickham. Men who take to gambling like those two have done do not heed their mistakes. I could pay his debts, but he would only accumulate more. I do wonder who he owes. If it is anyone of rank, he could be ruined."

"He will be ruined for his scheme against you," said Mr. Hurst. "He is digging his grave deeper with every move he makes."

Elizabeth squeezed her eyes closed and sighed before she reopened them. "Thank goodness my sister is safe. What if he had followed through and married her? What sort of life would she have lived?"

"I have removed Bingley and Caroline from my home. When they departed, one of my footmen followed them to the Clarendon."

"The Clarendon!" An incredulous bark burst from the colonel's throat. "He certainly thinks well of himself. You would think he would economise—retrench."

"I have heard the dinners are four pounds a person," said Hurst, "and if he wants wine with the meal, the claret is an extra guinea. I cannot imagine how much he will spend living there with Caroline. I am certain she will order wine and champagne whenever she feels the urge. No one ever told that woman 'no,' but someone should have. My servants were ecstatic to see her go. The butler told me they made punch to celebrate."

Elizabeth lifted her eyebrows. "And you let them?"

"Madame, I joined them," he said with a laugh. "I plan to take my wife to the country. We shall not be a part of the Season. I need to ascertain her intentions in regard to her family and our marriage."

"What would you have me do?" Fitzwilliam's tone was low, and his countenance was serious, yet not hard. He was too good—to be concerned over Mr. Hurst's reputation in the matter!

Mr. Hurst knocked his fist upon the strong mahogany of the desk three times while he shook his head, then dropped his hand to his side. "Do what you will. I am certain I shall see word of it in the gossip columns. I shall decide how to act from there."

Lady Catherine! Elizabeth gasped, her hand flying to cover her mouth.

Her husband bent closer. "What is it, Elizabeth?"

"You gave your aunt directions to Mr. Hurst's this morning."

A smile cracked Mr. Hurst's stony countenance. "Do not fret. She did indeed appear at my door, but I informed her I had removed my sister from my home and gave her the direction to the Clarendon. She congratulated me for my good sense to throw off such an "artful harlot" and departed. I do wish I could have witnessed that set down." He clasped his hands and rubbed them together. "Forgive me for bringing you such news on your wedding day. I shall go. I do not want to intrude any more than I already have."

"I shall walk him out," said Colonel Fitzwilliam, "and I shall speak to both of you before the ball."

Elizabeth sagged upon their leaving. What more would be thrust upon them? Poor Fitzwilliam! He thought Mr. Bingley his friend, only to discover he put his monetary comfort before his relationships. She startled from her thoughts when Fitzwilliam tugged her from the chair, brought her to the sofa, and pulled her into his lap.

He yanked at the tips of her gloves until each finger gave enough to remove the entirety. "No more thoughts about Mr. Bingley or his horrible sister. If we could simply forget they ever existed, I would be satisfied."

"But if Mr. Bingley never existed, we would not have met," said Elizabeth as he began the same action with her other hand.

"I choose to believe we would. Richard would have still brought me to your uncle's warehouse. I know I would have seen your fine eyes and been entranced."

"Such pretty words, Mr. Darcy." She wrapped her arm around his shoulders and relaxed against him. "I do wonder, however, if you would have acted upon the enchantment. You seemed quite disinclined to the notion in Meryton."

"Peace! I will stop your mouth," he said before he kissed her. Gone were the sweet, gentle first presses of the lips. Had she tempted him beyond reason in her uncle's study? He nibbled and suckled in a manner unknown to her, and his hands stroked her arm to her shoulder, leaving pebbled flesh in their wake.

Her fingers clenched at the soft curls near his nape while she became lost in him, the silkiness of his tongue against hers, the tickle of her nose at the scent of his heady cologne, and the way he inhaled as his palm covered her breast.

He tore his mouth from hers. "Perhaps we should retire to our chambers?"

"Not just yet." She made quick work of his cravat, unwinding the long swath of fabric with a smile before she dropped it on the floor.

"What are you about, Mrs. Darcy?" His hand clenched around her thigh while she stroked along his neck.

"I am comfortable here and have no desire to remove myself from your lap just yet." Her eyes followed the path of her fingers as she untied his shirt and drew apart the lawn while he shifted beneath her. "Do you not want me to touch you?"

"Yes, I... You can touch me whenever and wherever you want." He reached into her hair and withdrew a pin. "I am yours, Elizabeth." He removed two more, and her long locks fell down her back. "Good God! I have imagined you thus so many times. My dreams pale in comparison to the reality before me."

He crushed her lips to his, groaning into her mouth while his fingers went to work on the fastenings of her gown. When the restriction of her stays released, she untied the ribbon at the top of her chemise. She had never been so desperate for anything in her life as she was for the touch of his fingers against her bare skin. As soon as she was nude from the waist up, she took his hand and pressed it to her breast.

He pulled away. "Elizabeth," he said in a hoarse voice. His eyes strayed from her face for but a second, and whatever he meant to say seemed lost. Instead, he stared at her breasts while his fingertips traced gentle circles that sent a current through every bit of her flesh. Her heart beat in an unnatural rhythm while she all but panted. How could he take control of her body as he had?

She needed a distraction! The buttons on his waistcoat gave way easily, and she worked at his shirt until it eventually came free, allowing her to caress those parts which had been hidden from her.

Without warning, he lifted a bit and laid her back on the sofa, stripped off his coats and shirt, inviting her to touch him. "You are not afraid?"

"I am nervous of what I do not know." She held his steady gaze while his hand slid up her leg. "But I am not frightened of you—I could never fear you."

"You feel so incredible." The words were nearly moaned when he rested himself atop her. His lips found a sensitive spot at the base of her neck while his hands made a careful exploration of the top of her thighs and her buttocks before venturing between her legs. Determined to trust him, she squeezed her eyes closed and let him lead her where he may. His fingers teased and stroked, making her gasp and whimper. Her one leg cradled his hip. She needed to get closer to him, but the room seemed to spin, so she gripped whatever she could to remain anchored somehow. Just when she could take no more, she reached what had been looming out of grasp, shattering into pieces as he covered her mouth with his to swallow her cries.

She could not move, could not so much as lift a finger. He drew himself up to his knees and ripped at his breeches. Her eyes fluttered closed while she tried to breathe. How did someone survive such an experience?

When his comforting weight settled upon her, she opened her eyes and cradled his face in her hands. He was so handsome. He kissed her thumb and bent to claim her lips in soft kisses. She attempted to press closer when his fingers returned between her legs stroking and teasing until something began to press inside. The stretching stung, so she gritted her teeth while he whispered against her ear. "I love you so much." He kneaded her thigh while he continued until he stroked her cheek. "Open your eyes, my love." He loomed over her with his brows drawn a bit towards the middle. "Are you well?"

"Is that it?"

"No," he said, panting. "I merely wanted to ensure this was not unbearable."

"Oh, no, I am well."

His head dropped to her shoulder as he began to move. He clutched her hips, digging his fingers around her hip bones as he guided her to meet him, teaching her the rhythm he must have craved. More than anything, she wanted to please him, but what could she do? She wrapped her arms around his slick back and buried her face against his neck. How could she keep from crying at the intimacy of the moment? Every moan and laboured breath made her pulse race and provided a satisfaction she had never experienced. Finally, a muffled bellow erupted from him, and he collapsed atop her, his chest and shoulders heaving.

She kissed his neck and his cheek while she trailed her fingertips up and down his back. Warm tears poured down her cheeks. Now she understood why her aunt had difficulties explaining what occurred between a couple on their wedding night. Yes, the act itself had been uncomfortable as her aunt had warned, but it was so much more. She could never have been so with anyone but Fitzwilliam. How could someone be so unfettered and vulnerable with a stranger? She had heard tales of it, of course, but that did not mean she understood.

When he rose to his elbow, Fitzwilliam's eyes widened, and she had to wrap her legs around him to keep from leaving her. "You said you were well. If you were in such pain—"

She stopped him by pressing a firm kiss to his lips, then replacing her mouth with her finger. "I told no falsehood. I am nothing more than overcome. Fitzwilliam Darcy, I am so happy to be your wife—in every sense of the word." She swiped at the damp upon her cheeks. "Pray, do not think this anymore than my silly emotions."

He kissed the paths of her tears. "I do not believe you silly. To be this way with you is more than I deserve—particularly since I took you on the sofa. Why would you not want to retire to our chambers?"

"Why, when I was content to be here? I had not planned to go quite this far, but I do not regret what we have done."

His arms wrapped tightly around her, then he shifted and rocked back, so she sat astride him. Free of his weight, she peeled her bedraggled gown and undergarments over her head. Her husband's intent gaze upon her form curled her toes. He found beauty in her body and that knowledge provided a boldness she likely would have never possessed otherwise. The gentle trailing of his fingers and his rapt fascination spoke louder than words.

"You are not shy at all, are you?"

"I never considered I should be." His muscles quivered under her fingers which forged a path down his stomach. "I suppose I am not much of a lady."

He frowned and tipped up her chin. "Why is that?"

"Because I love when you look at me. I feel beautiful and loved and…"

"And?"

She grinned and pressed herself to his chest. "And like you would devour me whole if you could."

He inhaled a shaky breath. "I most certainly would, but I must argue with you."

"Already, Mr. Darcy?" she asked in a higher tone.

"Yes, because you see, I think you very much a lady. In fact, you are the perfect lady for me."

Chapter 18

Elizabeth pressed her hand to Fitzwilliam's knee, ceasing that infernal bouncing. Was he always this ill-at-ease when attending balls? She caressed the top of his thigh until he grasped her hand and entwined their fingers. "If you continue, we shall return to Darcy House with the utmost haste, and Lady Fitzwilliam will be exceedingly put out."

She laughed and leaned against his arm. "I was attempting to calm your nerves. You were shaking the carriage."

"I do not anticipate a masquerade or ball at any time, Elizabeth, but my aunt has a scheme in mind for tonight." The equipage came to a halt, and he ducked down a bit to see through the window. "She would not willingly invite Bingley and his sister without some plan afoot." The door opened, and he alighted, extending a hand to help her down.

"I understand," she said once they made their way towards the door with her hand upon his arm. "I am not comfortable either." Miss Bingley and her brother were the least of her worries. What of the peers in attendance? How would they treat her as the new Mrs. Darcy? She heard her mother speak of the cruelty in the gossip columns on more than one occasion. She would manage, of course. After all, her courage always rose with every attempt to intimidate her, but she had no desire for her courage to be a necessity.

Fitzwilliam sighed. "Forgive me. You must be anxious over your acceptance as well as what will occur with Miss Bingley, yet you must know my aunt will not allow anyone to be rude to you."

As soon as their coats were taken by the servants, they were shown to a nearby drawing room. Lady Fitzwilliam extended her arm when they were announced. "There you are! I had begun to think you would hide away at Darcy House and I would be forced to send a few footmen to drag you here."

Elizabeth gazed about the room. Of course, she had heard of the wealth of the Fitzwilliam earldom. Who had not? But even though she had visited Wentworth House twice before, she could not accustom herself to the splendour. Thank goodness Darcy House was comfortable in all its elegance. She startled to Fitzwilliam giving her a nudge with his elbow, and curtseyed. "Good evening, Lady Fitzwilliam."

"You are lovely tonight, Elizabeth," said the countess, regarding her with a critical eye. "I do love your gown." She fingered the stitching upon the shoulder. "Your aunt said she had the perfect fabric, and I must agree with her."

"Yes, an associate of my uncle's imported the fabric from India. Aunt thought the colour would complement my eyes."

"As it does. And Madame selected a marvellous pattern for it." Elizabeth stroked her gloved hand down the front of her silk gown. The Cerulean blue contrasted with the white underdress, which gave a striking effect. "And I see Fitzwilliam gave you his mother's sapphires—an ideal choice."

"Thank you, Lady Fitzwilliam," said her husband.

"Lady Anne's favourite gem was a sapphire. Her father, the former earl, had the necklace and eardrops made for her, and your ring was a Darcy heirloom, as I recall." Elizabeth held up the hand that bore the ring Fitzwilliam had given her as a betrothal gift, a dark blue, round stone surrounded by diamonds. Lady Fitzwilliam glanced over her shoulder as Colonel Fitzwilliam entered.

"Darcy!" He strode forward and clasped his cousin's hand. "Mrs. Darcy," he said as he bowed.

"Pray, you must call me Elizabeth or Lizzy as my family does."

The colonel flashed a crooked grin. "Then you must address me as Richard." He rubbed his hands together and waggled his eyebrows. "Well? Are we ready for this evening?"

"I do not believe either of us relishes what must occur tonight." Fitzwilliam looked between his cousin and aunt. "Do you have a plan, or is this to be improvised as the situation unfolds? I must say, I believe a plan would be beneficial."

Richard waved his hands in front of him. "You need not know all."

"But—"

"Follow our lead," said his cousin. "We will manage everything, but know you are not to engage the Bingleys. If they approach, cut them."

His aunt dipped her chin ever so slightly. "My son is correct. Leave Miss Bingley and her brother to us. We have spent the days since your wedding devising this scheme, and 'tis not simple since we know not how either of the Bingleys will respond."

"Lady Fitzwilliam?" The countess turned to where the housekeeper stood in the entry to the servants' passages. "The guests have begun to arrive. Lord Fitzwilliam awaits you in the hall."

The countess took their hands. "Do not fear tonight. I promise we have taken every precaution. I shall send for you when the time comes." She motioned to her son. "Come Richard, you must greet the guests with us."

The colonel flinched and groaned. "Why? No one cares if I am present."

"With your brother and his wife in Yorkshire awaiting the birth of our grandchild, you shall stand in his place. Now come!"

Fitzwilliam's shoulders shook while his cousin trudged after his mother. "'Tis horrible, but I do enjoy when she treats him like she did when he was a child."

"But would you enjoy the experience if she did so to you?" Elizabeth clenched her hands and released them. "I must confess. I am not at ease."

As soon as they were alone, her husband stepped over to the tray of spirits and poured her a liberal measure of brandy. After he took a swallow of the amber liquid, he passed her the glass. "Sip this. We shall require our wits about us. It would not do for either of us to be in our cups." Fitzwilliam removed his glove and began trailing his fingers along the edge of her bodice. "My aunt is correct. You are stunning tonight."

With a step back, Elizabeth held up her hand. "Do not dare come closer. The last thing I desire is to be caught out or to need to beg a servant's aid to put my appearance to rights."

He gave her a rakish grin that made her warm all over, but she inhaled and took another two steps back. "I promise you may do as you wish when we are home."

His nostrils gave a slight flare. "Then we should depart straightaway."

"You know we cannot."

His shoulders dropped, and he sighed. "Damn Bingley for this! I never thought he could be so stupid—and manipulative!"

"Desperate people commit stupid acts." She rushed forward and pressed the glass into his hand.

Once he downed the contents, he slammed it upon the tray. "I want to be at home with you, in our bed where we belong."

"You do not believe we have spent too much time in our rooms since we wed?" She could not help the near giggle that accompanied the statement. After sneaking from the study in the middle of their wedding night, they sequestered themselves in the master's and mistress's suites. They had their meals brought to the sitting room where they dined in their dressing gowns, played chess, and spent every moment in the other's sole company. They had ignored their responsibilities and lazed about in the most decadent manner. It had been bliss!

"Fitzwilliam!" At Georgiana's cry, they pivoted around as she skipped forward and threw her arms about her brother's neck. "I hoped to see the two of you tonight. I have missed you both!" When she released her brother, she embraced Elizabeth. "Your gown is exquisite. Your aunt said she would take you to Madame de Beaulieu. Will you take me to her before I come out?"

"I am surprised your aunt has not taken you already." Aunt Gardiner possessed a few gowns by the renowned dressmaker, but Lady Fitzwilliam surely had a great many. Why would her niece not as well?

"Oh, no," said Georgiana. "My aunt and Mrs. Annesley agree I do not require such costly gowns since I am not out and since I seem to keep growing taller."

"Mr. Darcy, Mrs. Darcy, Lady Fitzwilliam is requesting you in the hall."

Georgiana jumped and covered her mouth at the interruption of the footman. "Oh!" She kissed Elizabeth's cheek then Fitzwilliam's. "Good luck! One of the maids has promised to tell me everything, so hopefully, I shan't miss a thing."

Elizabeth swallowed hard to rid herself of the burn in her throat and pressed her palm to her stomach. "I do not feel equal to this."

"I am of the same mind, Elizabeth. Just remain as close to me as possible." He handed her the mask he had placed upon the table earlier and donned his own.

She took his arm, clutching the wool of his topcoat, as they followed the housekeeper. "What if a gentleman requests a set of me?"

"Richard and my uncle should dance with you. After, I shall see if I can find those I trust." His hand covered hers as they entered the hall and approached Lady Fitzwilliam.

"The Bingleys arrived a short time ago," said his aunt as they neared. "That woman was asking of you, Fitzwilliam, before she even stepped foot inside the ballroom. For now, you will join us as we enter, my husband will announce your marriage, then you will join us in leading off the first set. My husband will also partner you for the second, Elizabeth." She pointed to their faces. "Pray, remove your masks for now. Mrs. Crawford will hold them until the first set ends. I want *that* woman to have an unobstructed view of your felicity."

"The musicians have sent word they are ready," said Lord Fitzwilliam as he glanced over his shoulder.

Richard clapped her husband on the shoulder. "Lizzy, will you dance the third set with me?"

"Thank you, Richard, I shall be honoured." If she did not have some distraction, and soon, she would be sick! How long would she be so on edge? The tightness was nauseating.

They entered the opulent ball room. Candles flickered from elaborate gold and crystal chandeliers, footmen mixed into the throng with trays of champagne, and a crush of people all wearing their finest of gowns and black coats crowded the enormous ballroom. "Ladies and gentlemen!" All heads turned to the earl, who stood at the top of the stairs, his arms outstretched. "Welcome to our annual Twelfth Night celebration. We are so pleased you could join us. Tonight, we celebrate not only the end of the Christmas season and start of the coming year, but also the recent nuptials of our nephew, Mr. Fitzwilliam Darcy."

The earl gave a half-turn and motioned back to them, prompting her husband to lead her forward to stand with him beside the earl and the countess. Meanwhile, the crowd murmured.

"We are thrilled beyond measure to welcome Mrs. Elizabeth Darcy to the family. Mr. Darcy, Mrs. Darcy, we wish you great joy and many happy years together." While he spoke, he and the countess took glasses of champagne and held them in the air as they turned to face Fitzwilliam and Elizabeth. "To Mr. and Mrs. Fitzwilliam Darcy!"

A footman held a tray of champagne in front of them as the occupants of the room raised their glasses. "Mr. and Mrs. Darcy!"

Elizabeth took a glass and raised it to the crowd, as did her husband before taking a sip. The bubbles tickled her lip and tongue while she sipped the crisp, dry wine. "That is lovely."

Her husband smiled while he watched her scrunch her nose. "Have you never had champagne before?"

"No," she said. "Papa would never go to such an expense and uncle is not fond of it."

The earl laughed. "Thankfully, your uncle manages to keep a generous stock. I mentioned my desire to toast you tonight, and he sent over three cases."

Elizabeth's eyes bulged. While the Fitzwilliams could certainly afford it, the expense made her short of breath. Would she one day take such extravagance for granted as well?

She and her husband followed Lord and Lady Fitzwilliam to the dance floor where she took her place across from her husband. The music began and he bowed to her curtsey before they started the pattern of the dance. She turned with the gentleman beside Fitzwilliam, returned to her place, and awaited another couple's turn while she grinned at her husband across from her.

"No! You do not deserve him! He was meant for me!"

Everyone in the room turned at the cry to Miss Bingley hurtling towards them. A loud commotion began, and Elizabeth was shoved from multiple directions as an ear-piercing wail joined the dissonant tones of the musician's instruments as each ceased to play.

Elizabeth gasped as she fell to the floor, the crowd swallowing her whole. "Fitzwilliam?" Where had he gone? A piercing pain shot through her shoulder as though it were being ripped from the socket. She scooted backwards in an attempt to free herself from whatever was pulling her. "Fitzwilliam!"

Chapter 19

Despite his unrest regarding the evening before him, Darcy's chest swelled at the sight of his of wife standing across from him in the line. She was all a lady should be—all his wife should be. Those in attendance watched her, some whispering to those beside them. Perhaps they saw the same intelligence and sparkle in her eyes that captured his notice in Hertfordshire? Her immaculately created gown stood out, its rich, bold fabric catching the light in a way that accentuated the sumptuousness of the colour as well as the dark flecks in her eyes.

His fingers yearned to pull the pins from her ebony locks and let the cascade of curls fall down her back. Her maid's skill restrained them and created a style that resembled a Greek statue, a piece of silk in the same shade as her gown peeking through those raven tresses. She appeared every bit what a mistress of Pemberley should be. He was a fortunate man indeed!

The first strains of the music began, and the dancers honoured their partners. While he awaited those who stepped forward and turned together, he glanced about the room. His aunt had indicated the Bingleys had arrived, but where were they? After his uncle's introduction, he would have expected them to approach as they walked towards the dance floor, but they were not to be seen. A knot appeared in his gut as Elizabeth's bright smile beamed at him from across the line.

"No!" came an ungodly wail from behind him. "You do not deserve him! He was meant for me!"

When he spun around on his heel, Miss Bingley rushed headlong in their direction, her gaze latched onto Elizabeth as she shoved her way through those along the edge of the dancing. Miss Bingley raised her arm, so Darcy stepped back and to the side to intercept her before she could reach his wife. A searing burn ripped down his cheek before he could grab Miss Bingley's outstretched arm. "Miss Bingley, control yourself, madam!"

"No," she screeched. "You were supposed to marry me! My brother promised!"

He managed to ensnare both of her wrists while her bony fingers contorted into grotesque claws. "Then your brother lied to us both. I have told him from the beginning of our acquaintance that I would never offer for your hand. We have both been used very ill by him, if you ask me." Where was Elizabeth? Where was Richard for that matter? Darcy was desperate to look behind him. He needed to know Elizabeth was well—to see her with his own eyes.

His uncle grabbed one of Miss Bingley's arms, which allowed Darcy to concentrate on the hand that scratched the devil out of his cheek. He tried to peer over his shoulder, but Miss Bingley wailed and started to fight the restraint.

"Elizabeth!"

"Perhaps she has been trampled to death." Spittle flew from Miss Bingley's lips, her wide eyes creating a countenance that would haunt his nightmares for some time.

"Shut your cursed mouth," said the earl. "Where are my servants?"

All of a sudden, Darcy noticed Bingley. He stood along the edge of the throng with his jaw agape. As soon as he saw

Darcy's eyes upon him, he gulped and made to turn. "Stop him! Do not let him leave!" Two men unknown to Darcy took his former friend by the arms and held him while, like his sister, he fought against being held in place. Where was a footman? His arms were beginning to fatigue.

His uncle stomped his foot directly in front of the woman and leaned closer to her face. "Cease this infernal struggling." Miss Bingley blinked, paled, then looked around at the crowd, who stared at her as though she were a show at Astley's Amphitheatre.

"I beg your pardon, sir, but we'll take her."

When Darcy turned, a footman stood at his side with three more behind him. Miss Bingley began to struggle and scream once more, but her antics did not prevent them from maintaining their hold of her and dragging her from the room.

"Mr. Bingley," said a man who approached. "I desire a word with you." Before he could argue, several men surrounded him and led him off in the same direction as his sister.

"Elizabeth!" Darcy turned back and forth, searching in all directions, but not a hint of her could be found.

"Here, Darcy!"

He ploughed through the guests in the direction of Richard's voice until those in his path cleared. When he reached his cousin, Darcy took Elizabeth by the elbows and bent forward to meet her eye.

"Is she injured?"

"She was knocked down, but I believe I reached her before she could come to harm."

"I did not know it was Richard grabbing my wrist." She teetered on her feet so Darcy scooped her into his arms and started for the closest drawing room. "Fitzwilliam, I am well. My shoulder will be sore, but no one trod upon me. I do not know how with the commotion, but they did not."

Richard glanced about. "I shall see what has become of everyone. Take her to the gold drawing room. 'Tis the closest, and it will be easier to find you when we have need of you."

After Darcy nodded, he hastened in the direction of the punch table, but stepped around it. "Pray, allow me to ensure you are well."

Her finger trailed down his still smarting cheek. "I should be the one ensuring you are well, my love. Are those marks from fingernails?"

He winced when her caress brushed over his stinging cheek. "I saw her rushing towards you and intercepted her before she could strike."

"Fitzwilliam, a few of these scratches are deep. We shall need to clean them, and well. I do not want you getting an infection."

He laughed and kissed the tips of her fingers. "As long as you are the one doing the cleaning." She rolled her eyes but wore a soft smile as they entered the drawing room, and he set her on her feet. "Do you have any pain?"

"As I said, my shoulder will be sore, but I am well." She pulled herself from his grasp and rang the bell. "We need to clean your face, and I do not believe your uncle would appreciate if I used the expensive brandy he purchases from my uncle for your wounds."

"Your uncle would not object."

She gave a light laugh. "He may. He manages a fairly steady stock, but even he will tell you obtaining brandy and champagne at this time is not a simple business." When a maid appeared, Elizabeth requested towelling and whatever liquor they used for medicinal purposes, and the maid hurried off.

Darcy wrapped an arm around her waist. "I could not turn to look or be of aid to you while I kept Miss Bingley at bay. Forgive me."

"Fitzwilliam," she said, cradling his face in her palms. "You restrained that woman and kept her from attacking you further, and likely, from assaulting me. You could not have known what occurred, and Richard was nearby. He removed me from harm's way without delay. No more could have been done."

His lips sought hers, seeking to steady the rhythm of his heart, which had been racing since she left his sight. She was in his arms and claimed she was well, but what more could be done to settle his disquiet? He deepened the kiss until a knock startled him, causing him to step back and turn his back to the door.

"Yes?"

The maid entered with a tray in her hands. "I beg your pardon, but here are the items you requested. The housekeeper suggested a bit of oil of lavender. I included that as well."

"Thank you," said Elizabeth. "We shall call if we require anything further."

As the girl departed, his wife pointed to a chair. "Now, sit there. I do not wish to raise my arms. Ladies' gowns are truly not made for such and are quite uncomfortable in that position."

He did as she asked, wincing when the alcohol-soaked cloth touched his cheek. "How deep are the marks?"

She met his eye and smiled softly. "Most do no more than penetrate the surface, but the base of some marks are deeper."

"Will you still think me handsome if they scar?"

Her head shook while she rolled her eyes. "You are ridiculous, but yes, I should indeed. You would be quite distinguished, though I do not think they are deep enough for that. Time will tell, however."

They both jumped when the door flew open, and the earl strode in, followed by the countess. "Of all the damnable things to happen! I must apologise to you, Darcy and Elizabeth. We fully intended to see them shunned. We also found to whom Bingley is most indebted and invited him as well. I had no idea when Evelyn and I concocted this scheme that the woman was truly fit for Bedlam. I know I joked of it, but I thought her behaviour nothing more than a scheme."

"Pray, do not let what occurred trouble you. We do not hold you at fault." Darcy lifted his eyebrows to Elizabeth, who looked over her shoulder.

"You are not at all at fault. If you had not arranged for us to announce our marriage before so many, she may have come to Darcy House. Tonight helped those who were not aware of Miss Bingley's delusions to bear witness to their extent, freeing us from any blame of her being jilted or me bewitching my husband."

"Good Lord!" Lady Fitzwilliam tilted Darcy's head. "That woman did that?" After she handed Elizabeth the oil of lavender, she stepped back. "Well, now she is locked inside a bedchamber with a guard at every entry and a physician has been called, as has the magistrate."

"The brother is in the library with Viscount Lisle," said Richard as he entered. "The viscount seems to have purchased all of Bingley's smaller debts to add to his own. I assure you that the puppy will have nothing in his coffers by the morrow. He will be lucky if he maintains ownership of his mills in the north."

Darcy struggled to keep his jaw from dropping. "He is handing over his debt willingly?"

"Not at all. The viscount offered to transport him to Marshalsea, and Bingley began to cry and beg. Then Lisle indicated he would not let up on the pup until the debts are paid. His dream of becoming landed is over, ruined by his own hand."

Lady Fitzwilliam's nose crinkled. "If his sister is sent away, he could sell her jewels. I doubt anyone but the ragman would care for her gowns, and I am sceptical of even that. She has a rather singular sense of fashion."

"I hope the ball is not ruined," said Elizabeth.

His aunt laughed and set her hands upon Elizabeth's shoulders. "My dear girl, do not concern yourself with that display out there. As soon as everyone was removed, the dancing resumed, and people began to gossip of what occurred. My masquerade will be the talk of London for months. I could not be more pleased—not that I planned for such a scene. I thought you would cut Miss Bingley, and I had all of my friends poised to cut her as well. I expected her to raise her voice, but not inflict physical harm. For that, I feel I must apologise."

Darcy stood and embraced his aunt, kissing her cheek. "You need not apologise. I do believe Miss Bingley would have attempted something regardless of whether she learnt at this ball or otherwise, but whether you object or not, we would prefer to return to Darcy House. You have announced our marriage, the Bingleys are done, and I would like to spend the rest of the evening with my wife in peace." With no argument from his relations, he took Elizabeth's hand and led her to their carriage.

He wrapped them both in rugs and drew his wife to his side, kissing her temple. "What do you wish to do when we arrive home?"

Her palm rested against his uninjured cheek. "I think I should love nothing more than to spend the evening in the library, curled in your lap, and kissing you, my dear husband."

He shifted as the sultry sound of her voice and the dance of her fingers across his thigh rendered his trousers uncomfortable to say the least. "Perhaps we should retire early? We would not want to spend the night in the library."

"Why not?" He groaned at her arch tone and single raised eyebrow. What had he ever done to be so fortunate? She pulled his face down beside hers and grazed her teeth along his earlobe. "As long as we have a fire to keep us warm, I shall be content."

"A sound observation indeed, Mrs. Darcy." He crushed his lips to hers, responding to her provoking words with an ardent kiss. Could a man expire from pent up desire? He stretched out a leg in an attempt to find a more comfortable position. His horses seemed to move at a snail's pace. Why could they not move any faster? He was quite impatient to be home.

Chapter 20

"I beg your pardon, Mrs. Darcy."

"May I be of aid, Mr. Cummings?" asked Elizabeth.

The staid butler held out several letters. "Mrs. Reynolds indicated you were to speak to Mr. Darcy. I hope you do not mind, but the post arrived a short time ago."

"I would be pleased to take those to him. Thank you."

"Yes, Mistress." Mr. Cummings gave a slight bow and disappeared into the servants' passages.

After the Twelfth Night ball, both she and Fitzwilliam desired to avoid the Season altogether and journey to Pemberley. They had left less than a week later and without speaking to anyone but the Gardiners and the Fitzwilliams. What a huge relief it had been to see the rolling fields of Hertfordshire!—at least until they had broken their journey at Longbourn. That would be the one and only time they ever stayed at her childhood home. Her mother mortified her, Lydia was brash and bold, and Mary quoted scripture until Elizabeth dragged Fitzwilliam from the house on one of her rambles for a respite.

At least now they were home at Pemberley, and, truth be told, she still could not credit she was mistress of such a vast estate. When she first set eyes upon the stone façade, gleaming in the afternoon sun, she could have fainted. She had never before considered the consequence of a man of ten thousand a year. How could she have known Pemberley was so grand? However, the more she learnt of Fitzwilliam, the more certain she was he appreciated her dim-wittedness on this particular subject. She had never fawned over him or spoke to him with any particular deference. She was free to be herself. How could she not be gratified by his appreciation of her?

She pointed to each door along the corridor. Which one was it again? Their arrival at Pemberley was a fortnight ago, and she still had difficulty finding certain rooms. The grounds were similar as well. Thus far, Fitzwilliam would not hear of her walking without a footman in the event she became lost in the forest. For once, she held her tongue rather than argue. Her father would never have believed it.

Ah! There was the marble bust of that rather unfortunate looking fellow! Fitzwilliam laughed when she described the sculpture in such a way but agreed. Once she knew her way around without using it as a landmark, she would have the gentleman stored in the attics. The expression upon the man's countenance could be quite terrifying. She could imagine Fitzwilliam and Georgiana as children walking on the opposite side of the passage to escape the man's evil stare. As soon as she sidled past, she knocked upon the door.

"Come!"

His countenance brightened the moment she stepped into the room. Once she closed the door behind her, she stepped around his desk and held the missives before her. "Since I was coming to see you, Mr. Cummings requested I deliver these."

He tugged her into his lap as was his wont. "What a brilliant notion. I much prefer to see your smiling face to Cummings's dour countenance."

"Fitzwilliam! He is not dour in the slightest."

After stopping her mouth with a noisy kiss, he took the letters and handed two back to her. "Did Cummings look at these? He handed you three letters for me, but two, in actuality, are for you." The neat and orderly handwriting of Jane stood out on the first, then she cringed at her mother's on the second.

"I shall read them later." She frowned at his sudden and serious mien. "What is it?"

"'Tis from Hurst." She leaned against him while he read, his arm wrapped around her and his thumb caressing her ribs. "His father was determined that Bingley and his sister would do no more damage than they had already wrought. Hurst and his father, under the supervision of a physician, drugged Miss Bingley and brought her to a hospital in Edinburgh. He says the place is not as crowded as Bedlam. They have little hope of her changing. For the time she was confined to her rooms after the ball, she ranted of being my wife." He looked up, his forehead crinkled. "I do wonder if Richard's jest of 'Spinster's Hysteria' was not wholly incorrect." He sighed and shook his head as his eyes continued to move over the page.

"Bingley was forced to pay out the remainder of his funds as well as sign over one of his mills. He also had to sign over his horses. Since departing London, he has retrenched to Scarborough and lives with a widowed aunt. Hurst and his father insisted Bingley manage his remaining mill himself, so he let the supervisor go and is doing the job himself. Hurst's father cited Proverbs."

"'Idle hands are the devil's workshop; idle lips are his mouthpiece.'" When he looked at her, she shrugged. "I have lived with Mary for almost nineteen years."

He laughed and bestowed a kiss to her forehead. "Hurst's father believes the occupation will keep him from further ruin."

"Let us hope," she said softly. "I am thankful Jane decided he was not the man for her. I could not imagine discovering such a deceitful character in my husband when I had no way to remove myself from the marriage."

Fitzwilliam kissed her temple then her hair. "We would have saved her."

"How?"

"At the moment, Bingley has no funds to travel or to bring a legal case against us. We would have simply brought her here to live with us."

She smiled at his thoughtfulness. "I had not considered he would have little recourse."

He sighed. "Hurst simply wanted us to know Miss Bingley and her brother were no longer able to do us harm. He has said Bingley is exceedingly quiet and flinches whenever our names are mentioned. Hurst's father threatened to have him hospitalised with his sister if he dared approach us. I would be surprised if we ever see him again."

"What of Mrs. Hurst?"

Fitzwilliam turned over the parchment. "Ah, here is a mention of Mrs. Hurst. They are forgoing the Season and spending the winter at his father's estate. Once the weather warms, he plans on taking her to the seaside for the summer."

"He is attempting to repair the damage to his marriage?"

"He does not say, but so it seems." Fitzwilliam tossed the missive onto his desk and entwined their fingers. "Perhaps I should send a note to your uncle. I could have a case of Port or brandy sent to Hurst for his trouble. The Bingleys may have been family, but he and his father could have done nothing more than turn their backs on them."

"I am certain my uncle would be happy to help. He would likely pay for part of the case himself. He and my aunt were quite severe upon Mr. Bingley's character, which was well-earned after his abandonment of Jane, but after he sanctioned his sister's dogged pursuit of you, my uncle thought him a most unworthy young man."

He released her hand to stroke her leg. "Enough of Bingley. I would be content never to utter or hear his name again."

She trailed her fingertips across his forehead, smoothing the creases, then down his temple and cheek. "Your aunt was wonderful to take Georgiana for the Season. I miss her, but I do enjoy having you all to myself."

He grinned and squeezed her hip. "As do I. I am only sorry I must take part of the day for business. I would prefer to spend all of my time with you."

"Perhaps I can be of aid?"

"You are meeting with Mrs. Reynolds and learning your household duties. I could not ask you to do more."

She wrapped an arm around his shoulders and began fumbling with his cravat. "Mrs. Reynolds does not need me. She can run this house better than I ever could. I have never met someone so efficient. I hoped you could accompany me to begin meeting tenants next week so I can contribute to something besides the menus."

"I shall speak with Mrs. Reynolds," he said.

"No, pray, do not. I cannot fault her for being proficient at what she does. She has run this house for a decade without the assistance of a mistress. I am certain we shall find a rhythm to our roles over time." She believed what she said. Mrs. Reynolds had been charitable and patient while showing Elizabeth how the household worked, which was different and more extensive than Longbourn. If only a quicker method existed for her to learn everything!

"We cannot walk today."

She lifted her head to glare at the clouds and rain pelting down upon the rose garden. "No, I know." They had been taking daily strolls around the gardens after luncheon. Due to the weather, he had returned to his study while she had practiced on Georgiana's pianoforte for a short time. "And even should the rain cease, the lawn will be too wet to walk on the morrow."

"Is this my wife speaking?" He drew back and stared. "The same lady who walked three miles in the mud to attend Jane at Netherfield?"

"Could you imagine Mrs. Reynolds' expression if I reappeared after a ramble with my hem drenched in mud and my boots as filthy as they were that day? The maids would never forgive me." The thought of Mrs. Reynolds' shock made her smile.

"I created many messes when I was a boy, and never did Mrs. Reynolds bear a grudge for it." Her fingers succeeded in working the knot out of his cravat and began to tug it from his collar, prompting a low laugh from him. "What are you about, Elizabeth?"

She grinned and slipped her leg over him, sitting astride his lap. "I thought we may take our exercise another way." When his neck appeared, she brushed her lips at the soft spot under his ear.

He groaned and clenched her thighs. "We have a perfectly serviceable bedchamber, not to mention a comfortable bed upstairs." As much as she enjoyed their moments together in their rooms, she loved surprising him, and even after almost three weeks of marriage, her willingness to seduce him in various rooms of the house never failed to shock him.

"I know," she said as she drew back from him and released the bib-front of her gown.

He dropped his head back against the chair while he kneaded her breast through her chemise. "You are wearing no stays, my love. You planned this?"

After nipping at his jawline, she nodded. "I even locked the door."

His hips lifted to rub against her. "Have I told you how much I appreciate the style of this gown? I do believe you should request a dozen or so from the dressmaker in Lambton."

She laughed, and he claimed her lips, swallowing her laughter and kissing her without one ounce of reserve. Their fingers worked at each other's clothing until they had enough exposed to be satisfied. She loved the manner in which he loved her, as though desperate to touch and savour every inch of her.

When they finally laid sated on the carpet before the fire, he looked at her bedraggled gown and his clothes strewn across the floor. "Now, how do you propose we return to our bedchambers? We shall never be able to put ourselves to rights before we depart this room."

Her eyes lit upon the door to the library, and she lifted an eyebrow. "Then we remain until everyone has retired."

"Elizabeth, that will be hours, and I assure you, we will be missed at dinner."

She laughed and pushed her husband, so he rolled to his back. "Then we do our best and hope we do not see any of the servants on our way." They helped each other dress, then Fitzwilliam peered into the corridor before he pulled her towards the stairs. Elizabeth clamped her hand over her mouth. She could not laugh lest someone discover them.

Fitzwilliam's lawn shirt was untucked and hanging about his legs and his waistcoat and topcoat were not buttoned. He would be mortified if they were found out. When they reached the family corridor, he opened his bedchamber door with haste and pushed her through, but she froze in her spot as her husband ran into her back. "Chambers?"

Elizabeth's free hand joined the first over her mouth. If she removed them, she would likely give a good impression of Lydia and dissolve into giggles. Meanwhile, her husband's valet hastened into the dressing room and closed the door.

She spun around but could not hold her laughter in another moment. "His countenance..."

Her husband joined her in her amusement. "I am thankful it was him as he will not say a word. You are just too tempting when you entice me as you did earlier, but we must be more circumspect. What if Georgiana caught us?"

She wrapped her arms around his neck. "I shall be more careful when Georgiana returns. I promise. If you like, we shall keep to our rooms."

His cheek pressed against hers. "Do not cease your attentions entirely. I must confess as to a certain curiosity as to where you will surprise me next."

"I love you, Mr. Darcy."

"And I love you too. I believe I had the best gift this year for Christmastide."

"What is that?" She had a suspicion what he would say, but she still wanted to hear it.

"You," he said simply.

Chapter 21

"Mr. Darcy?"

Darcy looked up from the ledger before him. "Yes, Cummings, what is it?"

"A carriage is approaching the house, sir."

He frowned, set down his pen, and rose, glancing at the clock upon the mantel. "'Tis too late for callers, and we are not expecting anyone until tomorrow." He tapped his foot a few times. Could it be? "Notify Mrs. Reynolds to heat water. I suspect our guests have come a day early. Miss Darcy and Mrs. Annesley will be with them so ensure all is in order. Apologise to Cook, but she will need to adjust dinner if at all possible."

"Of course, sir." With a bow, Cummings rushed off while Darcy walked to the music room where the happy notes of the piece Elizabeth was playing filtered into the hall. Between the master Mr. Gardiner had hired, as well as the time she had set aside to practice since they removed to Pemberley, she had indeed improved.

Her fingers abruptly stopped, and she looked up when he entered. "A carriage has been spotted upon the rise."

"Aunt and Uncle?" She stood and shifted from the stool.

"I suspect so. I sent word to Mrs. Reynolds when Cummings notified me."

"Thank you," she said as she took his hand. "Have you made much progress with your business?"

"Yes, a great deal. I know I should not have left it as long as I have, but I do not regret the reason for my procrastination." He grinned while she pinked just a bit.

"Well, I believe some of your distraction will be tempered with Georgiana's return."

He kissed the top of her ear. "I hope not." He spoke in soft tones and bit his cheek at the prickling of the flesh of her neck and shoulders. His chest swelled. How he loved that she still responded to him thus when he provoked her!

As he led her through the front doors to the steps, he relished her small hand in his, the manner in which her arm brushed against his, as well as that tiny curl that rested along her neck. She shivered if he kissed her there. He cleared his throat. It would not do to travel down that path, not when her uncle, aunt, Jane, and his sister would be arriving at any moment—but oh, how he wanted to!

"The weather is lovely today. Perhaps Aunt and Jane would like a walk in the gardens after dinner. When I was in the rose garden earlier, a few of the more unusual varieties were blooming. Jane, in particular, would enjoy seeing them."

"Did your aunt ever say why they chose to make their journey to the lakes now rather than August as they had originally planned?" His letters from Mr. Gardiner had contained nothing of that information.

"I confess I had wondered too."

"There!" He pointed to where the road appeared, and the stone bridge crossed the river.

His beloved laughed in that way he cherished. "I believe you are excited to see your sister."

"I have rarely gone so long without her company. I have treasured this time with you, but I am very aware Georgiana will not be with us much longer. She will be off and married herself, and I am certain sooner than I would like."

"You have some time left." Elizabeth looked up at him with an impish grin. "She told Jane and me that she wanted to wait to come out. After her experience with Mr. Wickham, she was in no hurry to find a husband."

He squeezed her hand and pressed his lips to her forehead. "I am being a sentimental fool, but..."

"But she is all you have other than me. Do not concern yourself. I do not take offence."

The carriage stopped before the house, the horses stamping and snorting. They still appeared to have a great deal of energy regardless of how far they travelled. As soon as the step was placed, Mr. Gardiner emerged and handed out the ladies, and a wide smile adorned his countenance when he turned and surveyed the house in front of him. "This is an impressive pile you have, Darcy."

"Uncle!" Jane rushed forward and embraced Elizabeth. "I am so happy to see you, Lizzy."

When he turned, Georgiana ran into him and wrapped her arms around his neck. "I have missed you, Brother. I am so delighted to be home."

"We are pleased to have you with us again," said Elizabeth as Georgiana threw herself into his wife's embrace.

Mrs. Gardiner curtseyed to him before hugging Elizabeth. "Another carriage with our servants and children should arrive soon. I love Jemima, Beatrice, and the twins dearly, but after two days sequestered in the carriage with them, I required a quieter journey today."

Elizabeth laughed with her arm wrapped around Jane's. "Oh, dear. Poor you! Why do you not come inside? I am certain Mrs. Reynolds will have tea awaiting us in the drawing room."

As soon as everyone was seated, Mr. Gardiner blew out a noisy breath. "I must beg your forgiveness for arriving on your doorstep a day early. You asked often enough in your letters what possessed us to change our travel from August to June, and then we decided to depart a day earlier than planned."

"We have indeed wondered—not that you are not welcome," said Elizabeth.

"I must confess it had everything to do with my sister. I always said father overindulged her and your father, well, you are well aware of how he copes with her behaviour." Mr. Gardiner wore a large frown, and his tone was low. He waved his hand. "She and Lydia were distraught over an invitation to accompany a colonel's wife to Brighton where the militia will encamp this summer."

At Elizabeth's gasp, Mr. Gardiner nodded. "I can tell we are in agreement over what a mistake that would be. Thankfully, your father put his foot down due to some information about one of the officers."

Darcy lifted his eyebrows to Elizabeth, whose shoulders relaxed a hair. When they had broken their journey at Longbourn, they had told Mr. Bennet of the evils of that particular officer. What a relief to know their warning was heeded. "I am relieved to hear of Mr. Bennet's decision, but what has that to do with your trip?"

"Your mother, with Lydia in tow, arrived at our home a week ago. She decided if Lydia could not go to Brighton, the two of them would spend a month complete in town."

"Oh, no." said Elizabeth before she covered her mouth.

Jane shook her head and sighed. "Mama has been terrible. Aunt and Uncle told her we were to depart for Derbyshire, but she would not listen."

"We decided to leave a day early and delivered your mother and Lydia to Longbourn on our way," said Mr. Gardiner. "The entire ride, she went on and on about how we had treated them ill. Your father was not pleased to have her back, but as far as I am concerned, he wed her. She is his responsibility."

"Pray, do not make yourself uneasy," said Darcy. "After all, I must beg your forgiveness for my aunt Lady Catherine's unexpected arrival."

"Hah! Your uncle and I were playing chess when she appeared. She is a prodigious amount of bluster and wind, but your uncle forced her departure with a swiftness I admire. You should apply to him if you wish to know what he did, particularly since she was prepared to journey here as soon as she could remove herself from the 'stench' of Cheapside."

Darcy sucked air through his teeth while Georgiana gasped. "I shall pen the earl a letter and thank him. Elizabeth and I are pleased indeed not to have been forced to endure a visit from Lady Catherine."

"Yes," said Mr. Gardiner, "I would imagine you are, but I assure you, she was no difficulty."

At a knock upon the door, all turned to Mrs. Reynolds as she entered. "I beg your pardon, but I just wanted to let Mr. and Mrs. Gardiner know the children have arrived with their servants. They are being shown to the nursery to refresh themselves."

Elizabeth stood and nodded with a smile. "Thank you, Mrs. Reynolds. Would the rest of you care to refresh yourselves and perhaps rest before dinner?"

"I would!" Georgiana sprang from her seat followed by Jane.

As soon as Mrs. Reynolds accompanied their guests up the grand staircase, Fitzwilliam pulled Elizabeth into the library, closed the door, and tugged his wife into his arms. "Whatever shall we do until dinner?"

"Do you not need to finish your ledgers?"

"I finished before Cummings entered. I am yours for the rest of the day."

His wife grinned and touched his cravat. "I like that."

At a tug to his neck cloth, he covered her hand with his. "I am not averse, but I have no desire to scurry to our chambers dishevelled. While I would not want Georgiana to see us, I would enjoy your uncle catching us even less."

She patted the front of the knot. "Very well. Shall we rest then?"

"I can guarantee you will not rest," he said in a near growl.

After she laughed at his tone, he drew her up the staircase and to the master's bedchamber. As soon as they were blessedly alone, he claimed her lips for a sweet kiss before dropping his head to her shoulder. "Have I told you how happy I am being your husband?"

Her fingers combed through the hair at his nape. "You have not said the words, but I am not blind to how much more you smile and laugh now as opposed to when I first made your acquaintance. I must say I am quite content to be your wife if you were unaware of my feelings on the matter."

He lifted his head and caressed his fingers down her cheek. "Should this be a dream, I never want to wake. I have never had a Christmas gift such as you."

"You still consider me your Christmas gift?"

He smiled. "Yes, the most perfect one I have ever received."

"You flatter me, sir, for I am far from perfect. You do remember how much I like to fall, which I have done already in the park." She had indeed tripped on one of the pathways and scraped her hands. "I am woefully unprepared to run this house, though I am learning, albeit slowly. I also have yet to fall with child, which, as my mother reminds me in every letter, is my most sacred duty to you."

After he brushed his lips against hers, he sighed. "If you fall, I shall be pleased and delighted to carry you all over Pemberley and the grounds. Mrs. Reynolds says you are doing well in learning all that is entailed in running this home, and hang your mother."

"What?"

His fingers began pulling pins from her hair, dropping them on the nearby dresser. "Our children will come when God determines it, and if they never come, I would be content to spend my life in the sole company of you. I shall have no regrets. Truth be told, I am satisfied with the time we have had to ourselves. I have no wish to share you too soon."

Her eyes shone with unshed tears. "You are the dearest man, and I love you."

"Good, because you are my entire heart. I cannot survive without you."

"Then, I suppose we should never be apart, which suits me well, since I could not survive without you either."

Fitzwilliam Darcy dropped his forehead to hers. Elizabeth was his wife, which made him the most fortunate man who lived.

The End

Acknowledgements

This book has been an interesting ride. I wrote a version of the first chapter years ago for the Pride and Prejudice: Behind the Scenes anthology for Austen Variations. At the time, a few people, as they usually do, suggested I lengthen it and publish it. The notion has always sat in the back of my mind, and when I was thinking I should write a holiday novel (I always enjoy a good holiday novel!), I pulled that old Word file out and began revising and continuing the first chapter. The rest came quite easily.

As always, I have to thank Carol S. Bowes for her amazing red pen and extensive Regency and Pride and Prejudice brain power. She keeps me on point and ensures I show and don't tell. I owe her more than I can ever afford to pay for the time and effort she puts into my books. They wouldn't be what they are without her!

To Debbie and Marie for their incomparable proofreading skills—thank you!

My dedication only tips the iceberg to the people I am thankful for lately. From those who offered their advice as to where to move in the local area, to those who have offered their help since the house started falling apart around us. I have had offers from wine and chocolates, to a DD, and my neighbors who help keep us in drinking water (and thankfully, keep us showered!) so we're not using that emergency water tank outside the house faster than necessary. It's been a crazy ride, but has shown me we have a lot of friends to be thankful for.

This is copied directly from the acknowledgements of Agony and Hope, but I still mean it. I couldn't think of a better way to say it! So—Lastly, to the fans who keep me going. I thank you for every post and message. On those days when I struggle to write, I have you in my head or even on my social media, telling me you're re-reading one of my books or which one is your favorite. Those may not seem like much, but when the words just won't come, your messages make me keep trying until the words are right. To quote Austen: "For you alone, I think and plan." Thank you for reading!

About the Author

L.L. Diamond is more commonly known as Leslie to her friends and Mom to her three kids. A native of Louisiana, she spent the majority of her life living within an hour of New Orleans before following her husband all over as a military wife. Louisiana, Mississippi, California, Texas, New Mexico, Nebraska, England, Missouri, and now Maryland have all been called home along the way.

Aside from mother and writer, Leslie considers herself a perpetual student. She has degrees in biology and studio art but will devour any subject of interest simply for the knowledge. Her most recent endeavors have included certifications to coach swimming, certifying as a fitness instructor and indoor cycling instructor, personal trainer, and corrective exercise specialist. As an artist, her concentration is in graphic design, but watercolor is her medium of choice with one of her watercolors featured on the cover of her second book, *A Matter of Chance*. She is also a member of the Jane Austen Society of North America. Leslie also plays flute and piano, but much like

Pride and Prejudice's Elizabeth Bennet, she is always in need of practice!

Leslie's books include: *Rain and Retribution, A Matter of Chance, An Unwavering Trust, The Earl's Conquest, Particular Intentions, Particular Attachments, Unwrapping Mr. Darcy, It's Always Been You, It's Always Been Us, It's Always Been You and Me, Undoing, Confined with Mr. Darcy, He's Always Been the One, Agony and Hope* and *His Perfect Gift*.

---

[i] Constantia wine is from the Constantia valley near Cape Town in South Africa's Cape Peninsula. Developed by Dutch settlers in the late 17th century, the aromatic wine possessed an intense and lingering sweetness and was considered among the top dessert wines of the world. It was also "little produced," which made it very expensive. So much so that it was usually purchased exclusively by the aristocracy and royalty of the world.

Sources: Fullerton, Susannah. *Contribution to Jane Austen's Regency World Magazine.*

Kelly, Pauline E. *Jane Austen Dictionary*. Ink Well Publishing (2009)

Shapard, David M. (editor). *The Annotated Sense and Sensibility*. Anchor Books (2011)

www.ingramcontent.com/pod-product-compliance
Lightning Source LLC
LaVergne TN
LVHW030911080826
845145LV00010B/2854

9781737335641